THE TROUBLE WITH EVE

FORBIDDEN FRUIT
IN A
BIG SKY PARADISE

RON NEFF Ph.D

THE TROUBLE WITH EVE
FORBIDDEN FRUIT IN A BIG SKY PARADISE

iUniverse books may be ordered through booksellers or by contacting:

iUniverse
1663 Liberty Drive
Bloomington, IN 47403
www.iuniverse.com
1-800-Authors (1-800-288-4677)

ISBN: 978-1-6632-0294-9 (sc)
ISBN: 978-1-6632-0295-6 (e)

Print information available on the last page.

iUniverse rev. date: 06/17/2020

For Everyone Who Believes in The Human Spirit . . .
and Heroes – both male and female
. . . especially in these trying times

ACKNOWLEDGEMENTS

The author wrote half of this novel before the Covid-19 virus largely shut down our communities. Like most people, he saw many of his friends very little – and some not at all – for over 2 months. But he was lucky. Six of them had already become characters in this tale. Hence, he could continue to see them in his mind . . . as each of their colorful personalities played out, every one of them adding delightful contributions to this heroic tale.

I say that with confidence, as **all** of my early readers remarked over and over on the "amazing" characters in this story, and were eager to read more about them.

Those amazing souls are Cory Sheetz ("TMK"), Jason Shepherd ("Rusty"), Jen Keith ("Jen-Jen"), Rob Rich ("Brando"), Stacy Keeler ("Stacy, the Indian Princess"), and Teresa Shephard (appearing under the same first name, as "Rusty's" wife).

Teresa earns double billing, as she also as served as the book's first editor. David Neff, my son, was the second editor and helped the book sail through the initial "content evaluation" with flying color colors.

1

THE BOOK OF GENESIS EXPLAINED
(OR: WHERE THE TROUBLE BEGAN)

What was that part about "forbidden fruit?"

Eve's new admirer had never been very attentive in Sunday school, truth be known. And maybe he was destined for HELL anyway, because Luka soon became skeptical of the whole religion thing. You were supposed to be a believer, he gathered, but he was a doubter. Yeah, maybe Satan had tapped him on the shoulder quite young – and tipped his scales toward eternal damnation way back then.

Or maybe Luka couldn't blame Satan. Maybe it was just his own inherent bent to be a doubter – a doubter and a bad boy.

"Let's hear more about that forbidden fruit," the bad boy was still thinking . . . even years later when he was trying to understand what he'd never believed in . . . trying to understand his own temptress.

Yes, Luka had been a doubter, even way back in Sunday school. They were SELLING something, he soon decided. And the evidence was clear enough, was it not? Just like any salesman, they were after your money. You barely got your butt down into a "pew" (one of those painfully hard, cold, too short in the seat and too straight in the back, wooden benches) before they started passing the collection plate.

Further, just in case you'd come in late (or had gone to the restroom? Or just hadn't given enough to buy your way out of eternal damnation and hellfire the first time?) they would pass that plate around again later, wouldn't they?

Hey, there was a logic to that sale, you know. You came in like the rest of the human sheep, just trying to stumble your way through life's trials the best you could, then . . . as the "service" went on, there were more and more devices (yes, that was the right word, Luka thought, "devices") applied, including hymns extolling and attesting to the wonders of the product they were selling, and a sermon that railed about the sordid and mournfully sorry state of humankind without that product . . . and/or promised you the moon, if you just suspended your doubt . . . just pledged blind faith . . . like a good boy should . . .

But what if you were a bad boy?

Here was the simple truth, Luka suspected. From the beginning, from that very first book of the Old Testament, that story of Adam and Eve, the whole thing was a sales pitch. It was a sales program designed to promote their product . . . your ticket to "salvation."

Even those dreadfully uncomfortable "pews" were part of the sales program. No matter how tired – or behind in your sleep – you might be, just TRY to grab a few winks in one of those torture devices, diabolically designed to keep you awake, a captive audience to the sales pitch.

Well, at least that was Luka's take on the matter.

Yes, her name really was "Eve." And Luka was sure of only one thing. She understood him better – a lot better – than he understood her. Was that the first rule in this game? (Yes, gentlemen, rule one: The woman is always ahead of you.)

But Luka did see one big UPSIDE. Many guys declared that "Women are all the same. They are all . . . (fill in your own adjectives here, if you're a male who subscribes to that view)." But Luka had found quite the reverse. In his experience, just like men, they were all different.

Now that might be the ONLY thing that women had in common with men. But – at least to Luka – it was a big PLUS. It meant he still had a chance – and dearly hoped that chance would be realized with the many-splendored Eve. She, he would swear, had set every cell in his body aflame with . . . with . . . what was it? Was it that? Was that the forbidden fruit?

Okay, he thought, if so, let it be. Let it be so . . . with Eve.

> And when the broken-hearted people living in the world agree
> There will be an answer, let it be
> For though they may be parted, there is still a chance that they will see
> There will be an answer, let it be
> Let it be, let it be, let it be, let it be
> Yeah, there will be an answer, let it be . . .
> Whisper words of wisdom, let it be
>
> (Lines from "Let It Be." Recorded by The Beatles. Released 1970.)

If this fire inside him for Eve was the forbidden fruit that had led both the creator's first human experiments to be cast out of paradise – to be thereafter just mortals, fated to die before long, and now awkwardly aware of their own nakedness; no longer creatures truly made in HIS image . . . Well, so be it. If that was the story, let it be . . . Luka was ready, even at that price.

Besides, he thought, everyone knew that girls seemed to prefer bad boys. Hey, if that's what it took . . .

What WAS that forbidden fruit? What was that literally unspeakable evil that Eve had (allegedly) tempted Adam with under the "tree of knowledge?"

In truth, that wasn't very well disguised, was it? Well, was it?

We all know it was that most sinful (but also delightful) fruit of her body. Yes, that irresistibly adorable body of hers. And, at this point, Luka was not thinking about that mythical figure in the ancient Garden of Eden. He was, once again, daydreaming (or was it "lusting?") over the charms of his own new love interest.

Okay, if he had to go to hell for it, maybe she was worth it, Damn it. Yes, Damn it, "Damn it to Hell," as the ministers sometimes liked to say.

And wasn't that a double standard? Why was it okay for THEM to say that?

So what were the facts? As noted above, Eve was allegedly tempting Adam with some literally God-forbidden – damnable (yes, worthy of eternal damnation) -- sin.

But Luka was thinking that maybe Eve should have had a good lawyer. After all, the evidence against her ... that what she offered was truly sin . . . was flimsy at best. Damned flimsy!

"What are you getting me for Christmas," Eve asked. "I don't know, you little vixen. Right now, I just want to give you a kiss . . . you look so delicious," Luka answered, smiling wryly and moving toward her.

Eve surrendered to his kiss, although not so fully as he would have liked, not a long, deep one . . . not a prelude to imminent love making.

"So what do you WANT for Christmas, My Sweet?" Luka asked after the all-too-brief kiss. "Well, Luka, you KNOW that," she offered. In truth, he didn't even know whether she really meant that remark or not. More likely it was just one of her little fake complaints. She really was a champion at those fake complaints.

"What I probably SHOULD give you is a good spanking," Eve's admirer suggested, provoking exactly the little pout she did so well. That pout, he knew, was also fake. She wasn't upset or forlorn. She was just messing with him . . . as usual. . . And, of course, he was fascinated with it all.

"I'll bet you'd really like to spank me, wouldn't you," Eve now countered – and with not a pout, but a coy smile and an oh-so fetching turn of her shoulder toward him.

"Damn. It just isn't fair," Luka thought to himself, "She's holding all the cards. She knows very well that I'd love to spank her cute little tail. Not hard, of course. Just with little love slaps – and lingering caresses on those beguiling curves."

Of course, that was all said only in his mind.

Not that she didn't already know that much, anyway.

Despite his seemingly bold and "in charge" remarks to try to keep her, if not off balance, at least not bored with him, Luka really didn't know what to expect from Eve. Nor did he know whether -- or how long – he could count on her attentions. It was touch and go; day to day.

One thing Luka COULD count on was his good buddy T. M. He was a big guy – big as a horse, and (to H with the religious types who might frown at the term) a real BAD ASS.

T. M.'s real name was Cory, but most people called him The Mighty Quinn, T. M. or TMK. Never mind that Quinn was properly spelled with a "Q." When they wrote it out, many of his friends spelled it "Kwinn."

No matter. TMK was easy going; hard to rile. That, Luka had noticed, just seemed to go with the territory. The really big bruisers were typically like that. It was the little guys who were always acting feisty; hitching up their pants and putting up their fists all the time, like they were itching for a fight.

Well, The Mighty Quinn was the biggest bruiser around. He looked like he could walk right through the side of a house, or just rip that side off, if the spirit moved him. From some of the stories that were told in the area, that was probably about the size of it.

In any case, no one gave T. M. any lip. If they didn't call him T. M., TMK or The Mighty Quinn, they just called him "Sir."

It was good to have a buddy like T. M. If you were his friend, any other guy would think twice before giving you any crap.

Luka had another good friend, this one a popular and refined lady, whose raised eyebrows were potent weapons. If some jackass – or tramp – was out of line, acting crude, her scornful glance could stop the offender right in his or her tracks.

That refined lady's name was Teresa, and she and Luka liked to give each other big hugs. Teresa was a world-class hugger, but it didn't go any farther than that with Luka. Why? Because she was married; married to another of Luka's good buddies, Rusty.

"To hell with this guy," Luka would sometimes say on encountering Teresa and Rusty . . . on the street, in a store, in a bar or elsewhere . . . then reach for one of Teresa's warm and wonderful hugs. Those hugs were good for him. Luka knew that much. Teresa seemed to love them just as much. In fact, if Luka didn't reach for her, she would ask, "Hey, where's my hug?" with her inviting arms open and ready.

Teresa also had large and in charge, "commanding" blue eyes. But more on that later.

As for Rusty, on the surface he was quiet and almost shy, it seemed. And he had the most innocent looking "baby face," as everyone said. Of course, people in the area knew that innocent appearance of Rusty's belied the facts. He was always up to something; always planning his next gag or other crazy trick. It wasn't clear whether Rusty did that to amuse himself – or to entertain his friends. Maybe it was both.

But right now Rusty, Teresa, Luka – and Eve, too – were all focused on another matter; something that had them all worried.

Luka had gotten the call late last night. It was a good thing that Eve's new admirer usually stayed up late, and nearly always answered his phone calls.

TMK was in jail. In jail for what, they didn't know yet. But he had called Luka for his bail -- and that bail had been set quite high, at $5,000.

What had riled The Mighty Quinn? Who, what and how ghastly were the damages? And how much trouble was he in?

2

OF THE BIBLE'S MISSING BOOKS
(OR: THERE WAS MORE TO THE STORY)

While many (if not most) religions seemed to base their sales pitch on a negative view of human nature – on painting the two-legged mammal as prone to nothing good (and hence sorely in need of their reforming product), it was easy to paint quite a different picture.

Luka liked to write sometimes, and he had written this:

> "When the seasons of mother earth have passed beyond the awakening wonders of spring, through the manifest glories of summer's robust foliage, thriving crops and noble beasts in their prime habitats, culminating in autumn's harvests, the trees adorned in multi-colored leaves no longer green but dazzling in their array of darker hues, and critters seeking places to "hole up" for a while, with most of the trees soon barren of leaves and seeming the Specter of Death, the landscape resigns to the dark and dreary days OF WINTER. . . . Yet it is exactly then that the human creatures rise to the occasion and produce their own elaborate decorations, and celebrations, complete with joyous songs and carefully prepared feasts of traditional delicacies to share -- the biggest holidays of the year!"

Aren't humans rather amazing, after all? Well, aren't they?

And some of those humans are still more amazing than others. It wasn't even Thanksgiving yet and Eve was already asking Luka what he was getting her for Christmas?

"Who is the judge?" Rusty asked. "We don't know, Jason," Teresa replied, in the tone of a schoolteacher telling a first-grader, with all due patience, that his question was a bit misplaced, not quite to the point of the lesson in progress.

Yes, "Rusty's" real name was Jason, but people rarely called him anything but his nickname, the one the rusty-haired fellow had enjoyed since he was knee high to the proverbial duck.

In calling him "Jason" just now, Teresa was sending a message. Everyone knew that. Luka, perhaps in his friend's defense, allowed, "We ALL wish we knew more about this mess. Hopefully, we WILL soon."

The motley foursome were in Luka's car, an old but stately Mercedes Benz. It might help, they had agreed, to arrive with "their best feet forward," as it were. Hence Rusty and Luka were in suits and ties, and both Eve and Teresa in their best Sunday dresses. In Eve's case, that was a notably less revealing and more reserved garment than her typical attire.

Reserved and proper Sunday dress notwithstanding, Eve still looked hot to Luka . . . but he was shaking that off now. TMK was in trouble. That was the pressing matter at hand.

"I hope he has a lawyer, a GOOD one," Luka thought aloud, as he drove toward the courthouse. "His uncle is an attorney," shared Eve. They all turned her way, but she added no more.

Well, well . . . maybe Eve knew something the others didn't.

Despite his primary focus on driving -- and driving carefully and well within the speed limits – so as not to attract more trouble, Luka stole another glance at his new heart throb. "Whoa!" he was thinking, "Is she SMART, too?"

Eve might be "the whole package," in terms of what a man might wish in a mate, but they were about to learn that The Mighty Quinn was still THE MAN.

It was cold in the courthouse. The building was old with high ceilings and huge but darkened windows at each end of the hallway, windows looking like they were designed to block out prying eyes – as well as any sunshine -- and it was that time of year anyway when little sunshine was forthcoming. Suffice it to say that this was not a cheery destination.

Somewhere in the building a door slammed, and Luka reached out to take Eve's hand, with Rusty following suit to take Teresa's. It was good to stick together in moments like these.

Luka was thinking, "Was that slamming door an omen? Did it foretell of TMK being headed for the slammer?"

But Luka kept that eerie thought to himself.

No one in their foursome had been to the courthouse before and they needed directions. Stepping into an office with lettering over the door reading, "Criminal Filings and Records," a woman who looked like she might be as old as the building itself asked, "Can I help you?" She then told them, "The only criminal proceedings today will be held in Courtroom 3. That's the next floor up."

The door of Courtroom 3 was closed, but another older lady sat outside it at a small desk, and from her they learned that there were other cases ahead of TMK's on the docket, and they were obliged to wait. How long they would have to wait, they had no idea. That lady was not given to chit chat, and said simply, "Every case is different."

Soon the lady at that little desk disappeared around the corner, and they were left sitting on two benches along the wall in that otherwise empty hallway, hearing the benches squeak on the floor's cold, marble-like surface with any slight movement they might make.

Luka's eerie and disturbing thoughts returned. And now all four of them were thinking along the same lines. That courthouse was spooky, morbid, bleak and dismal . . . a bit too much like an actual prison. Was this a taste of that end? Was this the road that would lead TMK to that big slammer, a maximum security prison?

A strange little man, oddly biting a pen held between his teeth even as he spoke, came out of the courtroom door to say, "The Sheetz case is next."

Yes, TMK's last name was Sheetz.

As the little man stepped to the side of the heavy looking courtroom door, now wide open, TMK's four worried friends filed in wordlessly. Seeing that the room was nearly empty, Luka led them to the front row of benches, those nearest the tables always reserved for the prosecutor, the defendant and the defendant's attorney, if any.

There right in front of them sat TMK and, yes, there was a well-dressed gentleman sitting beside him, and whispering into his ear. At least, they all thought, TMK did have a defense attorney present. So far so good.

From behind a large and duly raised bench reserved for the judge, a smiling fellow tapped a little gavel just once and only lightly. Then standing up, with his black robe fully apparent now, that presiding magistrate declared, "In the case of the people versus Cory Sheetz, all charges have been dropped."

Teresa let out an audible sigh of relief, and Rusty couldn't resist slapping his knee in delight.

Although Teresa frowned at her always impulsive and irrepressible mate for the knee slap, the judge seemed to take that gesture in stride – and added, with his smile growing much broader, "The plaintiff now wishes to publicly COMMEND Mr. Sheetz for his bravery and his quick-thinking heroic act."

At this point, a man at the back of the room, a man TMK's

friends had scarcely noticed upon entering, came forward. As he came forward, they saw that the man had his arm in a sling, and now he reached out with his free arm to shake the hand of The Mighty Quinn.

To make a long story short, it had been at once a misunderstanding – and a still another memorable example of TMK's immense strength; that and his big heart. The man now with his arm in a sling had been part of a chain-reaction highway accident. Dazed at the time and still confused for several days after, that fellow had misunderstood what had happened. All he knew was that TMK had shouted something at him through his car widow before throwing his car off the highway into the grader ditch – and not by hitting him with another vehicle, but by the amazing strength of his bare hands.

For the record, TMK had not been part of the chain reaction pile up. He had been coming the other way, and only stopped to help.

While his arm had apparently been broken in his own collision with a car that had stopped short in front of him, it was likely that the fellow now shaking the mighty one's hand had suffered some contusions and bruises in his tumbling car after TMK launched it off the road.

But that was not the story.

As the state troopers had finally sorted it out, and the victim had now come to understand, if not for that amazing feat of strength, the man now shaking TMK's hand would have been crushed to death in that chain reaction accident -- by an 80 thousand pound semi-trailer that, with tires screeching, unable to get stopped, had been about to slam into him.

Better to be a bit bruised by a tumble then smashed like a

pancake, a human pancake . . . not an appetizing picture, to be sure.

TMK's vehicle, a huge 4-wheel drive pickup truck raised on its frame by an after-market lift kit, just seemed to fit him, of course, and both Rusty and Teresa wanted to ride with him as they left the courthouse. Not surprisingly, they wanted to hear more about what had happened that day, the day of the chain-reaction accident – and what TMK had done.

For his part, Luka was now pleased to have Eve all to himself in his "MERK," as he called that stately old Mercedes. As was the style of its era, that vehicle did not have separated seats in the front, but one large bench seat, big enough it seemed for several people. Eve was sitting near the passenger side door in that spacious front seat now (all too spacious, for Luka's taste at the moment). "It's lonely over here, Eve," he offered as a plaintive gesture. "Please come a little bit closer, My Sweet. There's another seatbelt in the middle." And, like the gentleman he was, Luka stopped the car; walking around to Eve's side, opening her door and assisting her to undue that seatbelt.

Eve was actually quite taken with this gesture. She knew exactly what he was after, but he did it . . . so well.

Sure enough, soon Eve had slid to the middle of the seat, well within Luka's arm reach once he was back behind the wheel. In fact, after she had slid to the middle – now with his right hand on her knee -- Eve joined right in when Luka started singing a song.

That song said it all, and just so honestly.

> I'm in love with the shape of you
> We push and pull like a magnet do
> Although my heart is falling too
> I'm in love with your body . . .

Every day discovering something brand new
I'm in love with your body
Oh—I—oh—I—oh—I—oh—I
I'm in love with your body

(Lines from "Shape of You." By Ed Sheeran. Released 2017.)

Thanksgiving Day was upon them, and most folks were spending it with their families, typically with extended family. In truth, they were NOT all delighted with their families – especially certain jackasses found in nearly any such enclave.

Despite such downsides, on the whole, most human souls actually experienced a sense of renewal, an often surprising feeling of warmth and belonging at those traditional gatherings. A few researchers had found evidence that at least part of that was – by now – embedded in the human genome. Even if the individuals now present were not your favorites, the traditional rhythms of the season -- likely including the same holiday trappings, even the same menu items, from the turkey to the candied yams -- struck "home" in your DNA.

Did that make your slimy uncle _____ (fill in your own slimy uncle's name here) any less slimy and repulsive? No. But it may very well enable you to laugh that creep off – and so many more others you would encounter in the coming year – more placidly now, as per your renewed sense of vitality and belonging after sharing in those holiday rites and rituals.

There are so many songs, it's easy to borrow a few lines,

There'll be parties for hosting
Marshmallows for toasting
And caroling out in the snow

There'll be scary ghost stories
And tales of the glories
Of Christmases long, long ago . . .

There'll be much mistletoeing
And hearts will be glowing . . .

(Lines from "It's the Most Wonderful Time of the Year."
Version recorded by Andy Williams. Released 1963)

In accordance with all of this, Teresa had planned and prepared a Thanksgiving feast with all the trimmings, right down to the cranberry sauce. She had also invited friends and relatives from far and wide to share in that holiday spirit and its renewing wonders. Guests would be arriving soon . . .

But where was that crazy Rusty?

Teresa had sent Rusty off to the store for a couple of last minute items to add to the pre-dinner relish tray. But that was hours ago. He'd mumbled something about ice fishing, but surely he didn't mean today. Or did he?

3

The Sermon on the Mount Revised
(or: By Their Fruits and Fishes Shall You Know Them)

It was nearly noon and Teresa was hoping Rusty would be back with the relish-tray goodies soon, as their guests would start arriving before long. In extending the invitations, the hostess had said "mid to late afternoon" as the time she had in mind for the big meal. She was bearing in mind, of course, that most people like to sleep in a bit on holidays, and while some could be expected to arrive early, others were always prone to be late.

In any case, people would want to socialize, "catching up on each others lives," for a while, before they would be ready to sit down for the meal. They would also expect to find nuts, candies, cookies and other assorted treats to munch on while the turkey, dressing, scalloped potatoes -- along with the green bean casserole and other side dishes -- were still in the oven and/or awaiting their stints in the microwave.

After taking a glance at the turkey through the oven's plexiglass door, and hitting the switch to turn on the light inside, the hostess and "chef du jour" turned the temperature down a few degrees. Turkey wasn't fussy to cook, but there was no use cooking away all that white wine she'd added to the stuffing inside it.

Now, where was that Rusty?

A glance out the picture window facing their driveway showed no sign of the predictably unpredictable guy she had married. What that glance DID reveal was that it was starting to snow.

Teresa was a bit concerned about the snow, although so far it was only a few flakes; no accumulation to speak of. A quick check on her smart phone showed that – surprise, surprise – the weather forecast had changed since she'd checked it early that morning. They were now expected to get 1 to 3 inches by midnight.

Well, that wouldn't be so bad. People in these parts were accustomed to driving in a little snow. Besides, weather was weather. There was no use fretting over it. Like most people with good sense, Teresa knew she might as well just try to enjoy it – and the white stuff did lend a certain beauty to a landscape.

> Oh the weather outside is frightful
> But the fire is so delightful
> And since we've no place to go
> Let it snow, let it snow, let it snow
>
> It doesn't show signs of stopping
> And I've brought some corn for popping
> The lights are turned way down low
> Let it snow, let it snow, let it snow
>
> (Lines from, "Let It Snow! Let It Snow! Let It Snow!" Version recorded by Michael Bublé. Released 2003.)

About half the guests on the list had already arrived when Rusty showed up with the black olives and pepper jack cheese, just as Teresa had sent him out for. Of course, being Rusty, he also had a mess of catfish in tow, fresh from the pond of a neighbor.

"Hi Rusty," said his cousin Vern, "Good to see you." "Yes, Rusty, good to see you," echoed Vern's wife, Ella, "But Teresa was worried sick," she added in a halfhearted attempt to scold the predictably tardy fellow who just brandished his ever-ready smirk in response.

In point of fact, that last remark was patently incorrect. Teresa never worried about Rusty. Oh, she got miffed at him at times, but worry? About Rusty? Teresa knew what all of his close friends knew. Rusty could pull off about any stunt you could imagine, and get away with it -- clean and slick as the latest icicle to form on a branch of a tree in a pristine Alaskan forest.

People were often scolding Rusty, but always with a smile, as his antics provided undeniable – if sometimes also eyebrow raising – entertainment. Mark Twain once said, "Life without music would be like a wagon without springs." Well, people in his privileged circle realized that life without Rusty would be far too predictable.

Perhaps because he was a skinny little guy, and he also looked just so damned innocent, Rusty was everyone's favorite imp. Mischief just seemed to be his job. Besides, he had the natural charm of an oversized elf.

"Just thought we could use some of my neighbor's catfish – as a SPECIAL delicacy to add to our feast," Rusty announced to his assembled audience. "And these puppies ARE special. No bottom feeders here. Me and the neighbor toss out freshly ground corn on the top of his pond every day – even when we have to break the ice to do it. These little babies will taste as light and exquisite as Orange Roughy – once I fry them up."

Unbeknownst to most of his guests, Orange Roughy was a rare and accordingly pricey fish, harvested only off the New Zealand and, sometimes, Western Australian coasts, and served at high-end French Restaurants.

And, as usual, Rusty was right. Once fried, ever so lightly in his secret batter, bites of his specially cared for catfish – served on one of the pre-dinner relish trays – were yummy yum yum, and disappeared quickly; much preferred by the guests over any other appetizer offered that day.

TMK arrived at the holiday gathering a bit late, but he had brought a guest who more than made up for that. It was the first time anyone there had met his cousin, who was an instant hit – especially with the gentleman.

"Let me introduce my cousin Jen," The Mighty Quinn declared, even as he and she were removing their shoes at the door, shoes now tracking new fallen snow. With her dazzling eyes, cute as a button tiny nose, and equally tiny feet, now un-shoed and beguiling the eyes in bright red stockings, Jen was enough to give any guy with hormones a sudden foot fetish.

For his part, the way he was admiring her -- even as his face glowed in announcing her to the assembled crew -- one had to suspect that TMK would have liked to say that she and he were KISSING cousins.

Indeed, every guy there would have liked to say that of Jen.

Before long they would all learn that – kisses or no kisses -- Jen's little feet were as talented as they were fetching to gaze upon. They were DANCING feet. And she soon had them ALL dancing.

> We get it almost every night
> When that moon is big and bright
> It's a supernatural delight
> Everybody's dancin' in the moonlight
>
> Everybody here is out of sight
> They don't bark, and they don't bite
> They keep things loose, they keep 'em tight
> Everybody was dancin' in the moonlight
>
> (Lines from "Dancing in the Moonlight." By Toploader. Released 1999.)

Yes, Jen had brought the music – and in more ways than one. She had brought not only her gifted dancing feet, but her talent for playing the most danceable tunes. In no time at all, she had hooked her smart phone up to Rusty and Teresa's surround sound system, and they were all delighting at the rock tunes – new and old – that Jen was playing for them, every one of them as danceable as "When the Saints Go Marching In," as played by a street band in New Orleans during Mardi Gras.

> We are all traveling in the footsteps
> Of those that'd come before
> And we'll all be reunited
> On that new and sunlit shore
>
> When the saints go marching in
> When the saints go marching in
> Lord, how I want be in that number
> When the saints go marching in
>
> (Lines from "When the Saints Go Marching In." Bruce Springsteen Version. Released 2007.)

It was fair to say that "Jen-Jen," as her close friends often called her, was the star of the party – and this on her first occasion to grace Rusty and Teresa's friends with her presence.

There was only one person who appeared to be less than dazzled by Jen. For some reason, the sultry Eve, Luka's new squeeze, did not seem at all taken with TMK's cousin.

Jen-Jen's eyes were gleaming with their always wet sheen, seeming to reveal the depth of her warmhearted feelings. On the other hand, Eve's eyes seemed to be seeing red.

The snow had continued to fall and, once again, the weather forecast had proven to be sorely inaccurate. Rather than 1 to 3 inches by midnight, by 6:00 P.M. they had already received 6 to 8. Further, the wind had picked up, resulting in drifts 3 or more feet high, many of them on the roadways -- making local travel nearly impossible.

Someone had turned on the widescreen TV in the family room where most of the guests were now watching a weather report. Rusty could not contain himself at the irony of that.

"Pinpoint Weather Forecast," it said on the screen, while a smiling and attractive woman was speaking. She was bedecked with knee-high boots trimmed in what looked like fur at their tops, along with a long scarf hanging around her neck, apparently someone's idea of making the speaker appear READY for all the snow.

Well, if she was ready for the snow, it was ONLY AFTER THE FACT, thought Rusty.

"What a joke," the ever-sarcastic Rusty commented, before adding one of his trademark cackles. He continued, "Pinpoint Weather? Or Accu-Weather? All these programs make such glowing claims for themselves. We should SUE them for false advertising. They're about as accurate as flipping a coin: Heads it snows. Tails it don't."

That telling commentary, offered in conjunction with his mischievous cackling, picked up the spirits in the room, with several rounds of chuckles and laughter rising in obvious accord with that sentiment.

On a more positive note than the miserable weather the TV was now reporting, they were all relieved that no one in attendance that day had headed out into the storm, now looking ever more treacherous.

What looked especially nasty were the high winds visible by the bending trees and swirling white images on the TV screen.

But they didn't really need the TV report on that score, because they could hear those winds HOWLING at times right outside their own walls.

It was becoming apparent that they were all SNOWED IN – at least for the night. "Don't worry," Teresa announced, "We have plenty of leftover food. And there are lots of blankets and pillows in the closets. We will all be snug as bugs right here for now."

"Hey, let's try out my new POPCORN MACHINE," Rusty chimed in. "It came with several bags of different flavorings to add in with the corn. There's even a Canadian bacon flavor . . . and I can't wait to try the Tennessee Whiskey flavored one."

No one was alarmed by the snow – nor even the prospect of being snowed in for a day or two. It was Montana, after all, and they had all grown up with storms like this; just a part of life out in Big Sky country, as it was called.

That moniker, of course, was quite accurate. The skies in Montana ready DID look much larger than elsewhere in the nation. If you chose to stay there, making it your home, you also knew that Montana was not for the timid. Everyone assembled in that home this evening was a hearty soul. They would just pass the popcorn, and share some wine and whiskey along with it. "Alcohol," as they liked to point out, "was good antifreeze."

Although alcohol didn't freeze, no one really thought that alcohol was a good defense against a human body freezing to death. It was just FUN to say that. And that potent stuff, "the Devil's Brew," as ministers would sometimes label it, did tend to improve attitudes, loosening people up for more lively socializing.

Luka probably didn't need much "antifreeze" at this point. His heart was already afire – and his loins, too, were now heating up to a near boiling point as he gazed upon Eve, who was now sprawled across a large pillow on the floor, face down, with her round little buns quite pronounced in those skin-tight yoga pants.

One had to wonder: Did she KNOW the effect that was bound to have on Luka? If so, should that be held against her? Of course, that also brings up a fun and timely song.

> If I said you had a beautiful body
> Would you hold it against me?
> If I swore you were an angel,
> Would you treat me like the devil tonight?
>
> If I were dying of thirst
> Would your flowing love come quench me?
> If I said you had a beautiful body
> Would you hold it against me?

(Lines from "If I Said You Had A Beautiful Body {Would You Hold It Against Me}." By The Bellamy Brothers. Released 1979.)

Well, it was fair to say that Luka would never hold that display against Eve – not in the accusatory sense of that phrase. He DID, as you would only expect, wish she would hold that body against him.

There was no surprise in any of that. But Luka WAS surprised to find that DESPITE his utter attraction to Eve and her body, that epitome of "the forbidden fruit," he was also delighted by the abundant charms of TMK's cousin, Jen.

What a wondrous world it was!

It was just possible, of course, that Eve had noticed Luka's wandering eye stealing a gander or two at Jen-Jen. It was also possible that this was the reason for that steely ALMOST LIVID look that had come into Eve's eyes when Jen was dancing – and doing it so well.

That was certainly possible.

But there may have been more to it.

4

THE TREE OF KNOWLEDGE
(OR: SO KNOWLEDGE WAS A BAD THING?)

TMK had been spending much of the holiday visit attending to his smart phone. "Who are you texting, big fella?" Teresa asked at one point. Nor was their hostess the only one curious about all that time that TMK was devoting to his phone. "What's her name?" asked Luka. "Is she hot?" The mighty one just shrugged his shoulders, but his contented face was giving him away.

Finally Eve, who was more persistent than the others – and far more assertive than most females – sidled up to TMK, offered her most provocative eye batting over a rolled shoulder and said, "You're not fooling anyone, big guy. So tell us the truth: Is she as cute as I am?"

As Eve awaited his response with one raised eyebrow now only about six inches from TMK's mouth, he stood up, still with that contented look on his face – and said only, "A gentleman does not disclose any intimacies with a lady."

Now Rusty, sensing an opening, declared, "Ah ha! So you ADMIT there is a sweetie you have been texting! Do you have any pictures?" TMK was unmoved, seeming quite set and satisfied in his ways about the matter. "She's a lady. That's all I'm going to say."

That only added to everyone's curiosity, of course, but The Mighty Quinn would disclose no more.

By now it was Sunday morning, three days since the blizzard had snowed them all in. According to the news reports – as well as the information they could find on the Montana Department of Transportation website – most of the main highways were open now, but the less-traveled side roads were not. In THEIR cases, that was not the news they wanted to hear. Rusty and Teresa's spread was well off the main thoroughfares; out in "The Tundra" as locals often called it.

At some point soon they needed to try to make a run into town for supplies, especially bread, eggs and other staples. Rusty wasn't sure if his snowmobile could make it all the way into town on a tank of gas. "Maybe I can strap on a 2-gallon can of backup gas," he offered, appearing to be thinking out loud.

"Don't' worry," said TMK, "Daisy can make it through. And I filled her tank just before Jen and I came." Daisy was the name TMK had given to his high-clearance 4-wheel drive truck. That high profile provided by the aftermarket lift kit – as well as the "rice tires," as they were called, tall and relatively narrow wheels and tires – were not just for looks.

All in attendance HAD NO DOUBT. Like The Mighty Quinn himself, that vehicle could go pretty much wherever it pleased.

And that was that.

TMK had disappointed them a bit by refusing to divulge any information about the sweetie he had been texting. But he would not disappoint them on this more serious matter. TMK and Daisy would "bring home the bacon," as it were; the snowbound party would soon have the supplies they needed.

And bacon did sound like a damned good thing to add to that supply list. Man does not live by bread – or eggs – alone.

Maybe "Daisy" was a surprising name for TMK to give to his high-profile vehicle. But he had been a fan of "The Dukes of Hazzard" TV series, and especially of "Daisy," Bo and Luke Duke's cousin, after whom those delightful shorts she always wore would be forever called "Daisy Dukes." (The Dukes of Hazzard was an American action-comedy series that aired on CBS from January 26, 1979, to February 8, 1985. A big hit, it ran for 147 episodes, encompassing 7 seasons.)

Perhaps the bible had been right in a sense. While scientists would argue that knowledge is good -- indeed, it had led mankind out of "The Dark Ages"-- not everything needed to be known to the world. Some things WERE better kept to oneself. In particular, there was a code of honor known as "chivalry" tracing back to knights and noble ladies in the days of King Arthur and The Knights of The Round Table. Even if those tales of medieval gallantry were largely fictitious, they did set admirable standards. And, just as TMK had asserted in this instance, it WAS only appropriate for a gentleman to decline telling anyone about the intimacies he shared with his lady fair.

It was a gentleman's rightful DUTY to protect the lady's honor.

It could be argued that there weren't many gentleman left in the modern world. But TMK was one of them.

Thanksgiving had passed, Christmas was only 10 days away, and there was bright sunshine glistening on a pristine cover of new-fallen snow. That new snowfall was only about 3 inches deep and the roads had remained quite drivable.

With all that sunshine, Eve and her friends were delighting in those distinctive Montana scenes; vast and wide open views of seemingly endless spaces rimmed in the distance by majestic peaks.

Make no mistake, they were also taking in those scenes DIRECTLY – spending much of their days right outside in that picturesque world, rather than peering at it only through windows or on a TV screen.

Some of those outings were devoted to cross-country skiing, hunting or ice fishing. But the most popular pastime in recent winters was snowmobile runs. Of course, those snowmobiles were the best way to get around for any purpose out in the vastness, whether to check on livestock, hunt, fish, or any other endeavor. But RACING those machines was now the BIGGEST thing.

At one time, those snowmobiles – and especially racing them – had appealed almost exclusively to the males of the species. That time had passed. Now many of the ladies were every bit as into that go-fast fun as their admiring counterparts.

Go-fast? You might be wondering: Just how fast does a snowmobile actually go? The answer is likely to surprise you. If your snowmobile is a model for beginners, it will typically have a top speed of over 80 mph. Sports models, preferred by seasoned riders, go from 100 mph to a stupefying 128. Here is a specific listing of several of the most popular models:

- SKI-DOO MXZ X 850 E-TEC – Top Speed: 128mph on the speedo and 120mph on gps
- 2012 arctic cat XF 1100 Turbo top speed: 118MPH
- Polaris Assault 800 Top Speed: 112mph
- Ski-doo mxz 600 Top Speed: ~ 160 km/h
- Polaris Switchback Pro-S 800 Top Speed: 105mph/168kph GPS: 98mph/157kph
- 2014 Arctic Cat ZR 6000 EL Tigre top speed 87.94mph 0-60 – 4.38sec
- 2015 Arctic Cat ZR 6000RR top speed 82.82mph
- 99 rmk 700 Top Speed: 106mph on speedo
- 2003 MXZ REV Sport 600HO Top Speed: (stock) – 107mph(Speedo)
- 1997 XC 600 tripple – stock – Top Speed: 102mph with 144 picks on speedo
- 1998 ZR600 Top Speed: 99mph(speedo) with a 1.5 inch paddle track

- ZR500 – Top Speed: 90mph(speedo) with 96 picks
- Ski doo 850 Top Speed: around 118 mph.

(Source: https://firstsnowmobile.com/snowmobile-speed/)

If that surprises you, consider this additional point. People who RACE those things often MODIFY them to go even faster, just like hot rodders modify sports and "muscle" cars. Modified snowmobiles can often exceed 200 mph.

Not only did many of the ladies in snowmobile country – certainly including rural Montana – like to ride and race these "rockets on runners" but they had a natural ADVANTAGE in races. As any hot rodder knows, performance is all about power to weight ratio – so lighter is always better. And most adult human females are considerably lighter than their male counterparts; many of them MUCH lighter.

Eve was seriously into snowmobile racing. In fact, she was a local STAR. Some of that attributed to the fact that she weighed only about 105 lbs.

Jen weighed in at about that same light number as Eve. But, at least to this point, TMK's cousin was content just to WATCH those races. Her thing was music and dancing, not racing.

It was probably just as well that Jen did not compete with Eve in snowmobile racing. As it turned out, Eve had a REASON to be less than thrilled when Jen had shown up at the Thanksgiving gathering hosted by Teresa and Rusty. To all but Eve, Jen was a new face on the scene, but unbeknownst to the others, she and Eve had a shared history.

At one time both of those cuties had lived in Missoula. While not exactly a metropolis, Missoula was the second largest city in Montana, with a population of just under 68,000. At that point, Eve and Jen were still in Middle School. Both of their families had moved to Missoula for a time, attracted by high paying jobs at oil refineries there, during a boom in oil prices that had accompanied the nearly decade-long Iraq War.

Eventually that oil boom had ended and their families – never really happy with city life, anyway – had moved back to their rural roots.

That much was fine with both of these young ladies. On the other hand, while still there in Missoula there had been a "love triangle," and not a happy one. As was common in Middle Schools, Eve had attached herself to a "boyfriend," at least in her own eyes. It was never clear whether the boy in question shared Eve's feelings in that matter. In reality, of course, at that tender age most boys were much less interested in these things than the girls, who matured earlier.

Here was the problem: Eve's supposed boyfriend had started giving lots of attention to Jen. He teased her all the time and would just stand there smiling at her when Jen said things like, "Grow up already, Rod." Yes, the boy's name was Rod.

To Eve, Jen had stolen her boyfriend. She had stolen his attentions. And that was NOT okay.

Bottom line: Eve would now be wary of any attention Luka might start to give Jen, her erstwhile nemesis.

One boyfriend lost to Jen was more than enough. Or, in the words of Great White, "Once bitten, twice shy."

I said my, my, my, I'm once bitten twice, shy babe
My, my, my, I'm once bitten twice shy baby
My, my, my, I'm once bitten twice shy baby

Oh, woman you're a mess, gonna die in your sleep
There's blood on my amp and my Les Paul's beat
Can't keep you home, you're messin' around
My best friend told me you're the best lick in town . . .
I said my, my, my, I'm once bitten twice, shy babe

(Lines from "Once Bitten Twice Shy." By Great White. Released 1984.)

To no one's surprise, Rusty had "hopped up" his snowmobile. Well, his new one. His last one had gone over a cliff, just before he'd dove OFF the thing to one side -- not being able to get stopped in time.

Oh well, everything has a downside. And snowmobiles are not known for good braking.

Besides, Rusty was not much into slowing down . . . for anything. Now with after-market modifications on his NEW "sled," Luka's radar gun had clocked him at 196 mph.

Not only was Rusty into EXTREMES, but girls had next to nothing on him in terms of their light-weight advantage. He weighed in at only 118 pounds himself.

That light weight was not just an advantage for acceleration and top speed, it was an even bigger edge for cornering.

Out on the open "tundra," cornering was not much of an issue, but Rusty was into more than just blowing across the expanses under those big Montana skies. He was into competition – and that meant racing on tracks; some of them circular, some of them oval; but all of them putting a premium on your ability to corner.

Right now Rusty was practicing on his own track; a makeshift OVAL one he had laid out for himself on his spread. He had entered the competition to race at the county's big event next week. And that would be on an oval track.

Tonight they were all going to watch Rusty during his time trials at that county track.

It was NOT a given that he would even be among the competitors in the race next week. You had to qualify.

If you qualified, then your starting position was determined by your elapsed time in comparison to other qualifiers. What you wanted was to be toward the front at the start, hopefully in the first row, and on the inside.

Rusty was new to this track – and hence whether he would qualify was uncertain at this point.

On the other hand, they could all be certain that one competitor WOULD qualify. That would be Eve. Luka's main squeeze was the local star on every track in the area.

As for Jen, she would just be happy to watch, as usual. There was only one complication. Jen was expecting a visitor this weekend, and he would accompany her in attending the race.

That visitor's name was Rod.

5

. . . AND HE THAT WATERETH SHALL BE WATERED ALSO HIMSELF (PROVERBS 11:25)
(OFTEN TRANSLATED AS "A GENEROUS PERSON WILL PROSPER.")

One of the advantages of living in rural America was that family -- including EXTENDED family – was taken much more to heart. This advantage became only more pronounced on major holidays, especially during the Christmas/New Year's holiday season.

It was an irony of the modern world that the more people per square mile, the fewer close friends or relatives people reported. Surveys had shown that for years. Indeed, people in densely populated urban areas viewed their neighbors primarily as threats, and were buying more and more security devices to PROTECT themselves and their possessions, many paying monthly fees to "ADT" and other security services to monitor their homes and report directly to the police at any sign of a break in or other trouble.

By contrast, people in rural areas would often leave their homes entirely unlocked – and even told their friends and neighbors they did that. Why? As a generous benefit to someone in need; be that someone they knew or even a stranger. "What if someone's car broke down?" they would say. "Or what if someone crashed a snowmobile or had a hunting accident, or maybe ran off the road trying to dodge a deer?"

And such things DID happen. Sometimes a rural dweller would come home to find a note on their kitchen counter or dining table, a note reading, "Thanks for leaving the door open," and adding perhaps, "I helped myself to a can of soup and some bread. Here is $5 to cover that."

Of course, if you told this to a person who had lived his or her entire life in a big city, they would think you were either daffy, living in the past, or trying to feed them a line of bull.

Yes, there were different worlds.

If neighborly ways – including generosity – were realities in rural areas, the importance of FAMILY was even more evident. There was an OBLIGATION to be hospitable and outgoing toward your kin. Sometimes that was experienced as a bit of a burden (when a particular relative was not much to your liking), but most of the time it was a joy. And the joy ran both ways. You were glad to see that extended relative, and they were just as glad to see you.

On the other hand, one thing about those extended family involvements ran much more one way than the other. For whatever reason – especially on major holidays – people in rural areas were unlikely to visit kin now living in cities. Instead, the city folks were more likely to visit their rural counterparts. In many cases, of course, that was partly a matter of returning to their roots . . . if only temporarily.

It was just such an extended family visit that brought Rod to visit for the holidays.

Luka was out on a service call; an after-hours service call. That was not unusual for him. Partly as a matter of neighborliness – and partly as a matter of necessity in these sparsely populated areas – it was only typical for a business owner to respond to a customer's call well after his supposed 5:00 o'clock closing time.

As was also typical of such rural areas, Luka's shop served multiple purposes, consistent with its longish name, "Barron's Plumbing, Heating, TV, Appliance & Electronics."

Luka had not started the business himself, but had inherited it from his father. This wasn't as routine as it might seem. Indeed, until his father's untimely accident, Luka had NOT planned to take over the business. Instead, he had hoped to become a computer programmer and make his living building websites.

That, he thought, was the cutting edge of everything now, clearly the wave of the future.

So much for plans, however. A person had to do what needed to be done. Someone needed to operate that business now, for both his family's sake and to meet the needs of all those customers. And, just as it had been when his father was the active proprietor, that store/shop still provided a wide breadth of products and services.

In a sense, that made Luka something of a "Jack of all trades." Was he also "A master of none," as the old adage had put it? Well, he hoped not.

In any case, Luka wasn't given to worry or fretting about such mundane things. The only thing that troubled him about being out late on that service call this evening was missing Eve's time trials at the county track. He had no doubt that she would qualify – and likely earn a prime starting position for the upcoming snowmobile race. He just didn't like not being there WITH her. After all, she was a hottie, and some other dude might try to horn in on his time.

The results of the time trials were in. Eve had made the front row and second to the inside.

Most of those in their circle were more interested to see what Rusty would do. First of all, he had next to no experience racing those crazy machines. Second, they knew he had a spanking NEW one, and well . . . he WAS Rusty.

Rod was now there with Jen in the hospital. It could have been worse. Rusty only had a concussion, not, as they first suspected, a skull fracture.

In his time trial lap, Rusty had actually MADE the first corner.

So far so good. Of course, as was nearly always the case, the track was not a true "oval" but two long straightaways with half-circle corners at the ends. As was also standard on such tracks, the trial lap had started at the "pits," located midway on one of the straightaways. There wasn't time to get up to a lot of steam before that first corner.

Things would get more interesting. After he had rounded that first corner, Rusty's hopped up machine could really show its stuff on the full straightaway ahead of it, something resembling that 196 mph it had recorded out on the tundra.

Rusty was determined to turn in the fasted "hot lap" ever recorded on that county track . . . which explained his current stay at the county hospital.

None of this surprised anyone in their circle. It was hardly the first time that Teresa's husband had appeared determined to kill himself trying to do the impossible. And it had started long before he'd met Teresa. According to an old song, some are just born to be wild.

> Get your motor runnin' . . .
> Lookin' for adventure . . .
> Take the world in a love embrace
> Fire all of your guns at once
> And explode into space . . .
> Racin' with the wind
> Like a true nature's child
> We were born, born to be wild
>
> (Lines from "Born To Be Wild." By Steppenwolf. Released 1968.)

Once his status was downgraded from "intensive care" to "stable," Rusty was allowed to have visitors. But the hospital staff were thinking it was time to REDUCE his visiting hours. Why? Simply because everyone loved Rusty and he was getting visitors almost all the time.

Hey, by now his friends knew that Rusty seemed to be indestructible. But the man DID need rest – especially when he was recovering from blasting completely off that racetrack, not making the second corner, flying right over all the fans at that end, landing in the upper empty seats, and sustaining a major concussion.

Helmets, after all, could only do so much.

One visitor had been there each and every day waiting for Rusty to pull out of intensive care and be able to see her.

Well before the staff might put any limits on his visiting hours, this visitor would finally put her foot down. Rusty's penchant for surviving the impossible would likely continue to flourish, but his snowmobile racing days looked to be OVER.

Teresa's commandingly large blue eyes were stern now. Those eyes were already saying what her words confirmed, "Two wipeouts are ALL YOU GET. If you bring home one more snowmobile, I'm gone."

Jen's friend Rod was there visiting because of the holidays. He was staying with his Aunt Bessie in the evenings and dropping in to visit several other extended family members in their respective homes while he was back.

Rod's Aunt Bessie was a character in her own right, a rather bossy character, as many could attest. But that was another story . . .

Rod's visit was about more than the holidays. He was testing the winds. And that was true NOT just in the metaphorical sense. Rod was a balloonist. He was into piloting high-flying hot-air balloons.

The first piloted hot-air balloons, sometimes carrying passengers, pre-dated the earliest airplanes. The Wright brothers famously flew the first airplane – if only for 12 seconds, covering just 120 feet – at Kitty Hawk, North Carolina in 1903. The very first hot-air balloon flight was recorded into history fully 120 years earlier in Annonay, France. Two brothers demonstrated their invention before a crowd of dignitaries in 1783. That flight had no one aboard. At the time, there was concern among scientists that people may have trouble breathing at such lofty heights. But, within a month of the same year, those Montgolfier brothers were documented to provide flights with first a sheep, a duck and a rooster aboard, and then with a human passenger.

About a month later, two French military officers piloted a hot-air balloon flight from the center of Paris to the suburbs, about 5.5 miles. Lest there be any doubt about the veracity of that duel-piloted fight, Benjamin Franklin witnessed it, recoding the celebrated spectacle in his journal.

Of course, those early hot-air balloon pilots -- many of whom failed in their attempts, and did not live to tell of their feats of gravity-defying splendor – were all dare devils. So was Rod.

First it was Jen? Then it was Rod? Eve could not help but wonder if she was being chased – perhaps even mocked -- by her past.

In fact, however, this was not the same Rod as the one whose attentions -- years ago in Middle School -- were stolen by Jen.

But one thing WAS still the same. Although previously just

a friend of the family, after spending a little time with her, this NEW Rod was now becoming quite taken with Jen.

It had started at the snowmobile time trials Jen and Rod had attended together. Nearly everyone in the stands that day was fascinated, either by Eve – who WAS both the star and a hottie – or by Rusty (who might do almost anything). But NOT Rod. His attentions were quickly captivated by the wonders of Jen.

That girl had grown up, and, in Rod's eyes, she was "filling out her jeans" just right. She used to be just a scrawny little tag-along friend of the family, but now Rod found her simply . . .

> She used to look good to me, but now I find her
> Simply irresistible, Simply irresistible . . .
> She's a natural law, and she leaves me in awe
> She deserves the applause, I surrender because
> She used to look good to me, but now I find her
> Simply irresistible, Simply irresistible . . .
> Simply irresistible (She's all mine, there's no other way to go)
> She's unavoidable . . .
>
> (Lines from "Simply Irresistible." By Robert Palmer. Released 1988.)

Were Jen and Rod soon to be an item? Well, that was distinctly possible. But Jen, like Rod, was only recently introduced to the local scene, and she was being noticed by more sets of eyes than his.

Even TMK thought Jen was the cutest thing since baby pictures, and was wondering if it might be okay to hit on her, even though she was his cousin. Who made these damned rules, anyway? Cousins? After all, if you thought about it, Adam and Eve's children had no choice but to mate with their own siblings, brother with sister, now DID they?

But TMK was only wishing. He wouldn't really trouble his sweet cousin with his erotic attentions, surely to bring both he and Jen only scorn in the community.

The real threat to Rod's intentions – his true rival for Jen's heart – would come in the form of a local fellow who was also starting to notice TMK's recently arrived cousin. That fellow was a theatrical sort, both literally and figuratively. He was literally fond of theatre, and actually building his own open-air theatre out there beneath the Big Skies, in the shadow of one of the stunning Montana peaks. He was also something of a ham, and theatrical just by nature – always looking to entertain an audience, large or small.

That fellow's real name was Rob, but one of his teacher's had nicknamed him "Brando," after a famous actor of her childhood, Marlon Brando. There was little doubt that his teacher had had a crush on that famous actor when she was a child. In truth, of course, she had never gotten over that crush and still managed to find copies of old Marlon Brando movies to watch, now converted to a CD format.

Fair enough, Marlon Brando was a terrific actor – and certainly did cast a dashing, all-man figure on the screen. Further, her student, Rob, now known to most simply as "Brando," was definitely committed to the theater himself, and did bear some resemblance to his nickname's sake -- including those heavy eyebrows, a penetrating gaze, and a muscular yet cat-like grace in his body movements.

Jen would have choices to make. Let the games begin.

6

ORIGINAL SIN

(OR: YOU WERE BORN GUILTY, PILGRIM)

Original sin? That was the clincher, wasn't it? No matter what you did – even if you lived a life worthy of becoming a canonized Saint – you were guilty of being a sinner, bound for eternal damnation, unless you drug your little behind into a local church to get baptized.

Forget freedom of choice or anything like justice. Burn in hell forever – or get in there, bow down, put your money in the collection plate, and get cleansed of that original sin.

Luka had to hand it to them. That was surely the ULTIMATE sales pitch.

Despite her terrific starting position, Eve hadn't won the big snowmobile race at the county track. She had finished third. Did that trouble her? Not really. Instead, she was daydreaming about meeting Brando for a sexual "tryst," a secret rendezvous.

Oh, Luka was a fine man, and he performed well enough in bed; very well actually, and she did regularly have orgasms with him. But wasn't it odd, Eve thought, that it was only MEN who were commonly suspected of being polygamous by nature – wanting to have a harem?

Although she would never confide this to anyone, Luka's main squeeze wouldn't mind having a harem of studs.

That was another irony, wasn't it? Everyone knew that a woman could always have sex again, even after an orgasm; while nearly all men were "one and done." Yet it was assumed that women were naturally monogamous? It wasn't just TMK (with the hots for his "forbidden" niece). Eve, too, was asking herself: Who MADE these rules?

Luka had no idea that Eve would ever daydream about having a harem of studs, or EVEN about sneaking off for a secret rendezvous with one other guy, whether Brando or anyone else. If he HAD known that, he wouldn't have been overly concerned. What he knew was that Eve had a strong sex drive, much stronger than any other women he'd ever taken up with. And, to him, that was a GOOD thing. She kept him happy that way.

Luka also knew that his main squeeze was TOO SMART to ever act in such a forbidden way, regardless of any daydreaming. Just like TMK not acting on his sexual attraction to his cousin Jen, Eve would be too smart to bring the scorn of the community upon herself. And just like her strong sex drive, Luka felt he was LUCKY to have a woman who was clearly much smarter than average. Indeed, Eve had been a straight A student in High School

No, Luka was not worried about Eve fooling around on him. She might DUMP him at some point and take up with someone new. But that was always a risk when you were involved with a hot property like her. He'd known that going in.

At this point Luka was not thinking about the possibility of losing Eve. He had something else on his mind -- and it was something that would CHANGE his entire view of life . . . and how he wanted to live it.

Luka's doctor had just told him he had an inoperative brain tumor. He had been having dizzy spells once in a while. That had been going on for months. Now the results of the brain scan were in.

According to his doctor, Luka could be dead in 6 months -- or he could live another 20 years. But it was nearly certain that he wouldn't live much longer than that, making his effective life expectancy only the mid 40s, at best.

Luka had not yet told anyone about his recent diagnosis. He was still "in shock." In fact, his doctor had said to EXPECT to be in shock for a while – and that he shouldn't make any quick decisions. "Give yourself some time to let this sink in. Call me if you start to feel panicky or depressed. I can give you medications for anxiety or depression." His doctor had also given him a hot line phone number to call, if he wanted to talk to someone about this, day or night; someone who would understand; someone else who also had a shortened and uncertain life expectancy.

There was a "group" too, a support group that Luka could join; although he would have to drive into Missoula for that, a little over 100 miles one way.

At this point, Luka had told no one. His first thought was that he didn't want to suddenly be viewed as an object of pity, like a cripple or something. He had always viewed himself as a rugged and self-sufficient guy. And he intended to STAY that way . . . . In his own eyes; and everyone else's.

Would Luka tell Eve about this diagnosis? Maybe. But only if she agreed to tell no one else.

Rod had asked Jen to a local dance. It was billed as a "Charity Ball," to raise money for needy families – a source of funding for Christmas baskets to be delivered to the homes of the less fortunate, most often homes of single parents, usually single mothers. There were many places for such parents to sign up for the Christmas baskets; at all the churches and the local schools, as well as grocery stores and the Walmart.

The dance tickets were $20 per person, and Rod, of course, had paid for both his and Jen's tickets, despite Jen's protestations, which were only mild, to be sure. Jen was always mild about things. Never one to yell at anyone, or give them a hard time.

That was a perfect choice by Rod, asking Jen to a dance on what would be their first real date. Jen was a dancer extraordinaire. She LOVED to sashay those little feet in time with the music, especially good rock tunes. Yes, as Rod had hoped, Jen could hardly say no to that offer.

It was a doubly good choice. The hot-air balloonist was into dancing, too. And, as many knew, all good dates start with two souls having a blast together. Then they will look forward to the NEXT one!

Today's hot-air balloons – splendidly GIANT teardrops in the sky – are much safer than the nascent versions first taking to flight over two centuries ago. Most important, the balloon itself (called the "envelope") is now made of strong and durable plastic, instead of the heavy and flammable paper and cloth used in early ones. Sometimes it is asked, "What if a large bird, maybe an eagle, collides with that envelope in the air?" Well, the bird may be dazed a bit, but today's balloon envelope will simply flex and flex back, never damaged a bit.

The "burners," too, the heating source that provides the hot air – not just at the outset for lift off, but off and on as needed during a flight – are much improved over those of the ballooning pioneers. First, the burners are now made of much LIGHTER metals. Second, they are powered exclusively by liquid propane, the same substance commonly used in high-end outdoor cooking grills. In its liquid state, the propane is highly compressed, hence taking up little space. It becomes gaseous as released for burning. Not only is this compact and light-weight, it's also FAR SAFER than the early hot-air balloons that had to be fueled on the ground and started dropping unpredictably at the point of cooling -- or carried dangerous open fires aloft, threatening the flammable paper and cloth envelopes above the flames, and fueled by burning wood or coal. (Even kerosene, one might note, was not invented until 1846; three quarters of a century after the earliest piloted balloons.)

On the other hand, the third part of the hot-air balloon, the "baskets" (still called exactly that) continue to be made of wicker, just like the baskets on the earliest flying contraptions.

When soaring into the skies TODAY, hot-air balloons and their passengers are actually quite safe, provided only that they have a competent pilot. That proviso is nearly always met. First of all, by law, hot-air balloon pilots must be licensed by the FAA (Federal Aviation Administration). And illegal piloting is unlikely for the simple reason that these wonders are EXPENSIVE. You are investing upwards to $40,000 on more to own one, if it is one of the larger ones intended to provide flights for several passengers at a time. One intended to carry only the pilot and one passenger will set you back about $25,000. And remember, that expense is not for anything you need, but just for grins, just for the hell of it.

Nevertheless, it is fair to say that the BIGGEST investment is not the money, but the time and determination. It is a very complex – and demanding – task to LEARN how to pilot one of these beauties.

Rod had the money, the smarts and the required determination to be a competent owner/operator of a hot-air balloon, one at once up-to-date and as large as they got -- large enough to befit the famous expanses of Montana's skies.

As Rod knew, however, despite the piloting regulations and all of their modern technology, hot-air balloons still faced one serious – and often lethal – enemy. That enemy was power lines.

Luka still hadn't told anyone in his personal circle about his inoperable brain tumor. But he did call the hot-line number his doctor had written down for him. It was past 11:00 p.m. and Luka explained to the lady who answered that he had called mostly just to see if anyone would be there that late at night. "Yes, it's a 24-hour hot line," the lady said, "One of us will always be on duty." Somewhat relieved, Luka just shared, "That's good. I guess I'm still in shock . . . . It doesn't seem real. But, like the doctor said, I may need to talk to someone when it starts to sink in."

"Yes, it might hit you HARD pretty soon," the lady on the line answered. "Sometimes it's like that. But most of us find that it helps to talk to someone in the same boat at any time. What are you feeling NOW?"

Luka was hesitant. After a pause, he reported, "I guess I'm feeling like I got cheated . . . Does that make sense?"

"Of course it makes sense," the lady answered. You DID get cheated . . . And the second stage of the loss process is anger." Since Luka said no more, the hot-line lady continued, "It's okay to be angry. It's only natural . . . And it means you may be coming out of the first stage, coming out of your shock and denial."

Luka was trying to make sense of her words – and of his feelings. "WHY do you stay up late to take these calls," he asked. "Doesn't it just remind you of your own loss; something you'd rather not think about?"

"I understand that thought," came the reply. "But it doesn't really work that way . . . Later, after you make peace with your loss, you will take satisfaction in being able to help others. That's the way support groups work. And this hot line, to me, is just like an extended support group."

"What's your name, young lady?" Luka now asked. "Becky" she answered.

"Thanks, Becky. That makes sense. Maybe we will talk again soon."

Unaware of Luka's dilemma, life continued apace in the lives of others out there in his little world.

For one, Rod would continue "testing the winds" there on his holiday visit. He was seriously thinking about MOVING from Missoula out to the rural tundra. Why? Because there were very few power lines out there. It would be a much SAFER place to fly his hot-air balloon. Besides, it was truly beautiful out there. Ballooning was mainly an esthetic experience – something one did for the visual beauty it provided. And it was beautiful out there in the tundra ALL THE TIME; even just standing out in it, or driving through it, or taking photos that "knocked the socks off" the souls to whom you sent them.

And Rod was sure it would be even MORE beautiful out there – when looking down at the panoramic view provided from the basket of his balloon in flight.

TMK had a surprise. Well, that was something of an understatement. As he often did, The Mighty Quinn would, once again, ASTOUND his friends.

After picking her up at the international airport in Missoula, he was with Michelle.

They were driving around in Daisy, his high-profile, bad-ass, 4-wheel drive monster truck. But the truck was not the star just now. Daisy had been upstaged by Michelle.

His new love interest had just returned from Paris. They had met on an internet dating website, and Michelle was mostly of

French ancestry. She had always wanted to visit Paris. And she was still aglow with the delights she had enjoyed there. She was babbling away about the open-air cafes, the parks ("Just like they looked in Renoir's paintings," she vouched), the Eiffel tower, and much more.

But TMK was sure that Paris had nothing on Michelle. She was striking -- long and lean, with a face fit for an actress.

Being tall himself, that was just the way he liked them.

TMK could hardly believe that she was finally there . . . there with him . . . in his truck.

Further, Michelle had KISSED him the minute she had entered the terminal there at the airport; the minute she had deboarded from her flight; instantly dropping the flight bag she was carrying in her hand, so she could reach for him.

As they had waited in the baggage claim area for her other luggage, she had been physically attached to him almost constantly; either holding his hand, or clutching and petting one of TMK's powerful arms as he kept it wrapped around her slender waist.

He was nearly back to the tundra now, but TMK's friends could wait. Right now he had Michelle all to himself. And he intended to treat her right.

"There is an all-night diner coming up ahead, My Sweet," he reported. Adding, "You must be starving, and I've stopped there before. The food is wonderful. Far better than airport fare. It's like real home cooking."

"That sounds perfect," she said, with a soft voice he found as endearing as the voice of an angel on high.

Whoa . . . Luka was dizzy again. It was worse than ever . . . and he wasn't sure he could make it to his phone.

7

Yea, Though I Walk Through the Valley of the Shadow of Death. . . (Psalm 23:4)
(or: Live Like You're Dying)

As usual, Rusty was bored. Something was about to happen. You could see that by the glint in his eye.

Teresa had been looking for interesting things to tell the kids in her Sunday school class. Not more "God stuff," as her husband called it. Just some interesting things to tell them about their state. She thought the children should be proud of their home. She also knew that any GOOD teacher, Sunday school or otherwise, had to tell interesting stories . . . to keep the student's attention.

While nearly EVERY state claims to be "God's country," Montana is more distinctive – more "larger than life" and memorable -- once you've experienced it, than most.

On the internet, Teresa had found a list of "fun facts about Montana." Most of them were . . . well . . . less than scintillating. Among them:

> Montana is the largest landlocked state in the U.S.

> Montana's first capital was in Virginia City, but in 1875 the capital was moved to Helena.

Considerably better, Teresa thought, were these two items:

> Montana is the home of the largest Grizzly Bear population in the lower 48 states.

> On Highway 59, south of Miles City, Harry Landers has topped 1 mile of fence posts with over 300 Western boots.

The Sunday school teacher especially liked the last "fun fact," and shared it with her husband. "Hey, I can BEAT that," Rusty declared, and headed off in a gust of chortles.

No one could chortle like Rusty. It was the sound of a laughing -- if maniacal – genius of HIGH JINKS . . . about to strike.

Jen and Rod had been a hit at the Charity Ball. In fact, they had won the DANCING CONTEST, taking home a bottle of homemade wine donated by "Old Henry Dunstill," as everyone called him. Yeah, Old Henry was getting on in years, but he did make some mighty fine wine. Speaking of which, that very topic comes up in the song to which the two of them had strutted their stuff, their winning dance number, selected by Jen, of course.

> Jeremiah was a bullfrog . . .
> I never understood a single word he said
> But I helped him a-drink his wine
> And he always had some mighty fine wine
>
> Singin' joy to the world
> All the boys and girls now
> Joy to the fishes in the deep blue sea
> Joy to you and me
>
> (Lines from "Joy to the World." By Three Dog Night. Released 1970.)

Luka had made it to his phone. And by that time, the worst of the dizzy spell had passed. But he had called that hot-line number anyway.

It was only 10:00 p.m. this time, but it was still Becky who answered. Luka meant it quite sincerely when he said, "Ah, Becky. I recognize your voice. And I'm so glad that YOU answered."

To make a long call short, Becky listened closely, and finally, ever so gently, she coaxed Luka to call his doctor the next day. "I'll bet he can give you something to help with those dizzy spells. I can just FEEL that. . . . Sometimes you just SENSE these things."

Was Becky clairvoyant? Could she sense events before they occurred? Maybe or maybe not. But, at least in this case, she was right. Luka's doctor did have a remedy, an aid, to help reduce his dizziness symptoms. It wasn't a pill or a shot, it was an EXERCISE he should do every day.

His doctor sent him home with a printout of the flowing instructions:

To do the Brandt-Daroff exercises, follow these steps:

1. Start by sitting down on the edge of a couch or a bed.
2. Lie down onto your left side, turning your head to look up as you do so. Try to do both of these movements within one or two seconds. Keep your head looking up at a 45-degree angle for about 30 seconds.
3. Sit up for 30 seconds.
4. Repeat these steps on your right side.
5. Do this four more times, for a total of five repetitions on each side.
6. Sit up. You may feel dizzy or light-headed, which is normal. Wait for it to pass before you stand up.

"While it might look a little complicated at first," Luka's doctor assured him, "It will soon become routine. And it only takes about 10 minutes each session."

He added, "You only need one session per day. But more won't hurt."

Sure enough. Luka tried it, and his dizziness spells were much REDUCED, occurring only once or twice a day, usually in the evenings, after he had gotten up from sitting. And his doctor had also advised, "Just go slow when you first get up out of a chair, or out of bed. It's the first couple of steps that will be most likely to bother you."

Luka usually did these Brandt-Daroff exercises right after he had his breakfast. And with that regimen in his daily routine, he felt so much better that he was now determined to ACT on his new philosophy of life.

Eve's admirer had decided that, if he was going to have a shortened life, he was going to "go for the gusto" as often as he could. Instead of just dreaming about doing the things so many of us think about – but put off, or consider just TOO wild, he was going to GO FOR IT.

There was a song that seemed to sum up Luka's new outlook on life.

"When it sank in . . .

"I went skydiving
I went Rocky Mountain climbing . . .
And I loved deeper
And I spoke sweeter
And I gave forgiveness I'd been denying . . .
"Someday I hope you get the chance
To live like you were dying"

(Lines from "Live Like You Were Dying." By Tim McGraw. Released 2004.)

As many could attest, there was another local fellow who had pretty much lived his entire life that way . . . almost from the cradle.

There it was, right on the side of Canyon Point, one of the Rocky Mountains that adorned their own Flathead County. About one third of the way up the side of that mountain there was now a statement: "Montana. It's Not for Wimps."

That statement was spelled out in GIANT blue and gold letters, Montana's state colors. The size of the print was large enough to be seen by anyone driving on Highway 83.

Few people would notice, but much smaller, in blue below that bold statement was a hyphen, followed by "Rusty."

How in the world he had pulled that one off no one could imagine. Did Rusty CLIMB way up there, dragging some kind of painting equipment? Or did he drag those letters up there already painted? Or???? Well, one couldn't rule out ANYTHING, given the culprit in question.

If one were a good sleuth, it might have been shrewd to inspect Rod's hot-air balloon for traces of blue and gold paint.

But that was only speculation. Would Rod be a party to such an audacious project? Only the two of them would ever know.

Still, one thing was clear. Rusty had upstaged those Western boots atop the fence posts along Highway 59.

That bold statement now on one face of Canyon Point was not incorrect. It could well be said that Montanans lived by the motto, "Go big. Or go home."

Brando's project was a case in point. He was building a giant outdoor amphitheater in the shadow of Cathedral Peak, another of the 314 named mountains in the same county. (Yes, believe or not, there were – and are – 314 named mountains in Flathead County, Montana.)

Further, Brando had equally big PLANS for his creation. Upon the completion of that amphitheater, it was Brando's intention to start a holiday tradition. If his plan worked out, Flathead County Montana would soon host an annual theater festival during the holidays.

Just like a film festival, it would be a competition. It would be open to traveling theater companies from anywhere in the nation.

Unbeknown to most, there were still dozens of traveling theater companies in America. They usually performed during visits to one of the 75 resident theaters that are members of LORT (the League of Resident Theaters). Those resident theaters were operating in 30 states and headquartered in New York. Appropriately enough, that headquarters was located on Broadway – specifically at 1501 Broadway, Suite 1801.

Hey, if Utah could host the Sundance Film Festival (largest in the U.S.), Montana could host one of the largest theater festivals.

At least that was Brando's take on the subject.

Certainly, there would be much to ATTRACT people to Brando's envisioned theater festival. Flathead County Montana is one of the most picturesque – truly STUNNING – places in the world to visit. In addition to all those Rocky Mountain peaks, it is home to Flathead Lake, the largest freshwater body west of the Mississippi; as well as most of Flathead Valley, with over 219 miles of wild and scenic rivers. It's also only 30 miles from the entrance to Glacier National Park. And, yes, that park is open to visitors all year around.

Incidentally, neither Flathead Lake, the valley, nor the county were named after flathead catfish. Instead, they were all named after the Flathead Indian Nations. The Flathead Indian Reservation was created by the Treaty of Hellgate on July 16, 1855. Located on the Flathead River, it is home to the Bitterroot Salish, Kutenai, and Pend d'Oreilles tribes – also known collectively as the Confederated Salish and Kutenai Tribes of the Flathead Nation.

That Reservation is another amazing tourist attraction. It encompasses over 1900 square miles of beautiful forests, clear streams, and unmolested natural meadows. And, like most Native American Reservations, it offers both a splendid variety of handmade native artifacts, and a rich history. You will find smiling Native America faces there, waiting to greet, entertain, and inform you.

While Flathead Lake does not feature flathead catfish, it offers literally "much bigger fish to fry." Both bigger and more interesting than that lowly bottom-feeding catfish, Flathead Lake is TEAMING with lake trout, pike, yellow perch and whitefish, along with some rainbow trout, bass, kokanee salmon and bull trout. Bigger? Lake trout caught in Flathead Lake often weigh in at monstrous sizes, frequently exceeding twenty pounds.

Yes, Flathead County, Montana is an extraordinary place. But SOME things are universal.

The holiday season is the most frequent time for marriage proposals. Interesting enough, it is also the most frequent time when one partner (usually the woman) dumps the other, to take up with someone new.

Eve was 26 years old now and had never been married. As many an unhappy man could attest, that's about the time when a never-married woman is likely to be thinking that her clock is running out. If she dumps her current partner, it's usually because he hasn't yet asked for her hand in marriage.

She breaks up so she can test the marriage market elsewhere.

It was not surprising that Eve would now ask Luka, "How do you FEEL about me?"

Luka was no fool. He got the hint.

After a pause, taking time to choose his words carefully, Eve's admirer replied, "I am very ATTACHED to you, My Love."

That response was true enough, and Eve did feel somewhat reassured. But it didn't address the real question, did it?

As a matter of fact, for quite some time now, Luka had been planning for just this occasion . . . just that type of HINT from Eve.

Indeed, he had practiced his opening line on the subject. Namely: "I think we should talk about the future . . . OUR future. Do you want to have children someday, Eve?"

But that was BEFORE learning of his inoperable brain tumor. Now Luka didn't know what to do.

Should he TELL Eve about his shortened life expectancy? After all, that would not offer a promising future for her, either.

If he didn't tell her, would he lose her anyway?

8

TWO ARE BETTER THAN ONE
. . . (ECCLESIASTES 4:9)
(OR: YOU ARE MY REASON)

The story is told of a humble man in Ancient India who confided to the Buddha that he knew he was a ROMANTIC FOOL. While others seemed to pursue financial security, knowledge, or some kind of legacy to leave behind, he thought that what true lovers shared was the most wonderful thing, and the rest was not much at all. Came the reply: "Everyone who has shared that kind of love feels the same as you, my son. You're not so different; just more fortunate."

Luka couldn't remember where he had heard or read that story, but now that his life had become intensified by its diagnosed brevity – the fact that it would end too soon – he was weighing what really mattered to him. And what really mattered to Luka was his love for Eve. It didn't matter whether she loved him AS MUCH as he loved her. It only mattered that she KNEW . . . that he somehow convince her that it was okay with him if he died soon, so long as she remembered that he really DID love her.

Yes, Luka was going to tell Eve about his diagnosis. He would tell her soon, but he would have more to say than that. And he was studying on just HOW to do that right.

TMK and Michelle were pulling into the large semicircular driveway in front of Rusty and Teresa's house. There were already many vehicles there. Teresa had decided to host another party. It wasn't intended as a holiday celebration per se, just a Friday night get together – one made BETTER because there were extended family from the city now visiting as per usual this time of year.

Of course, Teresa also knew that TMK would be bringing Michelle – to show her off. And she wanted the party to be, at least in part, a warm reception for them both.

Michelle could hardly believe it when they walked in through the front door. Suspended from the ceiling in large letters stretched across the entire front room was a sign reading, "Welcome to the Tundra, Michelle."

Shy and quiet by nature, Michelle was wordless. Indeed, she put one hand up as if to cover her face; something she often did in what seemed like an effort to hide the blushing she was prone to on such an occasion.

TMK spoke for them both. "Thank you all. What a wonderful surprise!" Then, taking Michelle's other hand (the one not still covering her face), he led her to the kitchen. That maneuver served two purposes: 1) to gallantly rescue Michelle from all that attention, and 2) to find something for them both to eat.

His shy lady may not be, but like Rusty, The Mighty Quinn was always hungry.

It was funny how Rusty could eat all the time and stay so skinny. TMK, on the other hand, like the colossal brute that he was, probably HAD to eat a lot just to MAINTAIN himself; much as a horse will munch grass all day out in a pasture.

Speaking of the devil, while the others (whether gracefully or just not wanting to rile TMK) had stayed in the front room, Rusty, the other constant muncher in their circle, would soon join the still surprised couple in the kitchen.

Oddly, that mischievous imp did not reach for anything to eat. Or maybe it wasn't so odd.

"So T.M., THIS is the hottie you have been hiding from all of us. Aren't you going to introduce me?" Rusty said, with his most charming smile aimed in Michelle's direction.

"Okay . . . I guess it IS your house . . . . Rusty, this is Michelle," TMK reluctantly obliged his friend.

Reluctantly? Well, it WAS Rusty.

Now, away from the crowd, Michelle was no longer overwhelmed by her shyness, and extended a hand toward the host. But, being Rusty, he wouldn't just shake her hand. Instead, he bent to a knee, took her hand lightly, and turning it over, KISSED it in the manner of a knight kissing the hand of a noble lady.

"Don't be fooled by Rusty's innocent looking baby face," TMK commented. "This sidewinder is as ornery as they come."

TMK's warning notwithstanding, Michelle was actually quite taken with Rusty's chivalrous gesture. And that was fair enough, wasn't it? There was enough crudeness in the world. Even if only done as a ploy to gain her admiration, such a gesture was a pleasant surprise.

On top of the HUGE surprise of the WELCOME sign strung up for her, Michelle was starting to feel that TMK was right. These were wonderful people out here in what they called "the tundra."

After catching her breath, "Please to meet you, Rusty," was Michelle's response, one in keeping with her preference for decorum and propriety.

"Same here," replied the host. "Where are you FROM Michelle?"

"I'm from Kalispell, Sir," his demure guest answered.

Although Michelle comported herself as though she might be from Europe or the upper classes of Boston, Kalispell was the County Seat, only 33 miles away.

As they all knew, the name "Kalispell" was Native American, a Salish word meaning "flat land above the lake." A town of just under 20,000, the fair city of Kalispell billed itself as "The Gateway to Glacier National Park."

Back in the front room, there were other IMPRESSIONS to be made.

Although both Rod and Jen had extended family in the tundra, and hence were familiar with the friendly ways of folks out there, neither of them was yet a known quantity in Rusty and Teresa's circle of friends.

Teresa, always the hostess to go out of her way to make the newer ones feel accepted, was having a lively chat with Jen. "Good to see you again, Jen," Teresa had offered, "You were certainly a hit with that great music you played here last time. I also heard about you and Rod winning that dancing CONTEST at the Charity Ball. Are you a professional dancer?"

"No, no," came Jen's reply, "I just do marketing and promotions for beauty products." Teresa was quick to remark, "Well, I should have known. You certainly LOOK great." And, of course, beauty products were one of women's favorite topics to talk about, and those two were soon into a lengthy conversation.

Beauty products not quite being Rod's thing, he decided to amble around the room, looking to mingle — and maybe start a conversation with one of the local men.

Soon Rod was actually the center of attention in a circle of men. What were they talking about? Ballooning, of course. And those dudes had LOTS of questions. "If you DO move out here, will you be offering RIDES in your hot-air balloon?" one asked. Others wanted to know how much he CHARGED for rides, how dangerous it was, how HIGH they went, would he be offering rides all year round — or only in the summer — and so on.

Indeed, those guys were even more into talking about hot-air balloons than Teresa was into talking about beauty products. Besides, Teresa needed to give some attention to other guests, and soon Jen was momentarily alone.

That was exactly the opportunity Brando had been waiting for. "Hi, I don't believe we've met, My Lady," was Brando's opening line. Yes, "My Lady" was a rather "flowery" expression by today's standards, but that was Brando. He was always given to grand gestures and eloquent words — in the manner of a Shakespearian actor, or a natural "thespian." Nor would that characterization have troubled Brando in the slightest. He knew that the term "thespian" traced to Thespis, the fellow who, according to Aristotle, was the first person to perform on a stage in Ancient Greece.

In truth, Jen thought that Brando was a little much. She usually went for men who were . . . well, a little more subtle. But she didn't snub Brando or put him down. Jen would never do that. Besides, even if a bit much, she thought he was a specimen; a real HUNK to look at.

Someone started playing holiday music on Rusty and Teresa's mellow, surround sound system. The timing of the music was perfect, as Teresa had just brought out a large bowl of holiday punch, a bowl cheerily colored in red and green, which seemed to contrast well with the foamy pinkness of the punch the hostess was now dipping out into crystalline mugs.

> Deck the halls with boughs of holly
> Fa la la la la, la la la la (fa la la la la, la la la la)
> 'Tis the season to be jolly
> Fa la la la la, la la la la (fa la la la la, la la la la)
> Don we now our gay apparel
> Fa la la la la, la la la la (fa la la la la, la la la la)
> Troll the ancient Yuletide carol
> Fa la la la la, la la la la

(Lines from "Deck the Halls." Version released by Pentatonix in 2016. Originally published in 1862 and written by Scottish musician, Thomas Oliphant.)

Teresa had done it again. Everyone was into the gaiety of the gathering, and many were joining in to sing the "fa la las" now accompanying their shared conviviality.

Then came a knocking at the door. It was not a loud or disturbing knocking. To the contrary, the knocker had to repeat his beckoning several times before anyone noticed — OVER the music, the many toasts being offered by the guests to their hosts and to one another, and over all the delightful laughter.

Finally, Rusty heard the knocking and made his way to the door. It was a UPS delivery man, whose facial expression revealed a bit of weariness and perhaps some irritation at the delay he'd endured before Rusty had answered his knocks.

The host invited the man inside. "Hey it's COLD out there. Come on in and have some ANTIFREEZE," Rusty entreated the fellow, gesturing at the punch bowl and several bottles of assorted wines and spirits on the table.

"Thank you, no," the delivery man replied. "I have lots of miles yet to cover," then just left Rusty eyeing the surprisingly large package now sitting at his feet.

The return address was not ringing any bells in Rusty's mind.

Roger Whitfield
201 E. Main
Westchester, Wyoming

"Who was that?" The head of the house was now wondering. And what could be in that package?

Although the UPS driver was quickly on his way, making all his scheduled deliveries for that day was becoming dicey. Once again, the weather forecast had changed suddenly, and he was driving in more and more snow.

Out there in Western Montana, UPS delivery vans were equipped with rugged, deep-treaded snow tires this time of the year. They were also supplied with tire CHAINS that, if necessary, could be laid out, driven onto and affixed to the drive tires.

As the snow got deeper and deeper on the road, and the forecast on the radio was now predicting 6-8 inches by nightfall, the UPS driver — wisely enough — strapped on those chains and headed to the nearest UPS service center. The rest of his packages could wait, hopefully to be delivered the next day, as weather permitted.

Back at Rusty and Teresa's place, they too, were becoming aware of the snow, and most of the guests would soon head home early, as well. But not just yet.

The contents of that UPS package were something of a mystery to Rusty. But he knew what he needed to do. Carrying that rather large delivery into the center of the front room, he set it down on the coffee table, held up his hands in the "hush" gesture to quiet the merriment, then asked, "Does anyone know a Roger Whitfield?"

Heads shook all around. No one answered.

After a short pause, "Hey Rusty," called Teresa, "Just OPEN it. We all like surprises."

Upon taking out his pocket knife and opening the package in short order, Rusty pulled out what was obviously a helmet, a full-faced helmet. There was a hand-written note attached to the strap. After reading silently for a moment, the host soon read the note aloud for the benefit of ALL assembled.

My name is Roger Whitfield. As a fan, I was at the snowmobile race the weekend before last, when you sailed far up into the stands. I read on the internet later that you had sustained a concussion. I suspect that your throttle stuck. In any case, accidents DO happen. I represent All*Star Racing Helmets, the top of the line; used by NASCAR racers, Top Fuel Dragster racers, and others in the know. Let me present you with this helmet, free of charge, compliments of All*Star Racing Helmets. Wear it in safety.

Well, Rusty was OUT of the snowmobile racing game. But, as everyone there knew, he'd probably NEED that helmet for some other shenanigan he'd pull — sooner or later and probably sooner.

Some things never changed.

Apparently, one of those things was that EVERYONE loved Rusty; even if they had never really met him.

All assembled were impressed by that gift. But, as Jen commented to Rod (now back at her side), "That's generous of them. But it's also shrewd. Half the nation probably heard or read about that spectacular accident. That helmet company will no doubt make sure that the same news outlets know about this generous gift."

Jen knew marketing and promotions, and she was exactly right. Everyone in the room would soon hear "human interest" tidbits about this from various media sources. And sometimes the company's slogan was included in the story; "All*Star Helmets. Accidents DO happen. We've got your melon covered."

Two of the regulars in Rusty and Teresa's circle of friends hadn't made it to the party. They were both sitting home, and not together. They were each at their own residence, pondering each other – and the hard realities of love.

They had been invited to the party, of course, but just the night before Luka had told Eve about his inoperable brain tumor, and his unpredictably shortened life expectancy.

Luka had also said, "I know you are at the age when a woman is looking to get married before too long. And I had planned to propose to you soon."

Eve was in shock, and saying nothing. So Luka continued, "I don't expect you to marry a man who has no future, or at best a shortened one. You deserve much better than that."

Taking a deep breath, Eve's ardent admirer closed his statement – one he had spent much time thinking about – with this: "But know this, My Love. I have made peace with my shortened life, and I am also at peace in letting you go – to find someone who can be there for you. I am okay with all of that, so long as you KNOW – and remember – that I really DO love you. And if souls or ghosts or spirits exist, I will ALWAYS love you."

9

. . .Out of Darkness and the Shadow of Death . . . (Psalm 107:14)
(or: Which Way Now?)

"It's almost too perfect," said Jen. "It looks like the whole world has been purified by the snow."

Yes, that's what it looked like from the basket of Rod's hot-air balloon that day.

The latest snowfall had brought a good 5-6 inches of a fresh and pristinely white blanketing, now glistening in the sun. But all that snow had come down gradually and with little wind, and thus without much drifting. It was just normal winter weather for Montana folks, and the guests had all made it home from the party just fine.

Now Rod and Jen, up early the next day, were basking in the visual wonders below them; as Rod was treating the hottie of his eye to her very first balloon ride.

Yeah, make no mistake, Rod knew how to make a proper Montana impression. (Rusty was right. Montana: It's Not For Wimps.)

Flying a hot-air balloon in the winter was not much different than flying one in any other season, provided there wasn't a blinding snowstorm underway. Besides, NOW Rod knew that there were folks out there in the tundra who were interested in receiving RIDES.

At the party, it had been MEN who were expressing lots of interest in his hot-air balloon, including taking rides. But if Jen was impressed, Rod figured that she could generate plenty of interest among females, too. After all, Jen WAS a marketing and promotions professional.

No, Rod was not "taking advantage" of Jen; he wasn't treating her to this ride only to drum up some business. Far from it! He was smitten by Jen-Jen, and hoping to sweep her heart away.

Still, it didn't hurt to "kill two birds with one stone," as the old phrase aptly captured it.

Eve and Luka had both made excuses to the hosts for missing the party. Was it just a coincidence that both had said they were "not feeling very well?"

Upon hearing about those identical excuses, some of the guests had nodded their heads with KNOWING smiles. Yes, there was much suspicion that the couple in question had just preferred to spend the evening wrapped in each other's arms. They all KNEW how those two -- for well over a year now – had seemed unable to take their eyes off one another.

Unfortunately, the reality of Eve and Luka's situation was much less appealing. It was literally TRUE that neither of them was feeling well. And their malady was one and the same. Both of them were suffering from what we commonly call "broken hearts." In somewhat more psychologically accurate terms, Eve and Luka were each in the midst of "grief work." Grief, of course, is what we feel upon losing someone we love. It matters not whether that loss comes from the other person's death – or from a parting.

This particular parting was a very strange one, to be sure. In fact, because of Luka's medical condition, this parting had elements of both a "break up" AND an impending DEATH.

Adding to the hellishness of the case, this parting was NOT one that EITHER of them wanted.

Luka, having known of his condition for quite some time, had already decided his course of action. Eve, on the other hand, just having learned of Luka's shortened and iffy life expectancy, was still trying to decide what to do. Should she do what Luka seemed to be – so gallantly – encouraging? Should she take up with some other man; someone who could offer her a future together?

Well, maybe. Or maybe not. But right now she felt like she may not have a future either. She just might die herself.

The pain in her chest was nearly unbearable.

To put it simply, they don't call it a "broken heart" for nothing. It really DOES hurt like hell in your chest. (If this hits just a little bit too close to home for you right now, see R. Neff, "Goodbye, My Love: How to Mend a Broken Heart." 2016.)

And the more you loved the person, the greater that pain.

As so often happened, Rusty was getting bored again. But he was not one to complain. No one had to hold his hand or buy him a drink. Rusty thought of himself as a man of action, and he would solve that little boredom problem HIMSELF, and in short order.

Yes, Rusty had a plan. And it was logical enough, he thought. A person shouldn't be wasteful. There was no reason to let that top-of-the-line All*Star Racing helmet go to waste.

To make use of his helmet, Flathead County's most colorful daredevil had just bought himself a top-of-the-line SNOWBOARD. It was not only top quality, but a Park board, one designed for maneuvers in "terrain parks;" and specifically constructed for those who were into JUMPING – and getting enough "air" to perform tricks.

One of the best snowboarding terrain parks in the world was only 23 miles north of Kalispell, the county seat. But Rusty knew he had to WORK UP to that. Those terrain parks were not for beginners.

No Problem. The newest snowboarder in the county would start by building his own little park . . . right there on his and Teresa's spread.

All that snow they had been getting was good for SOMETHING. What materials were required for building a good snowboarding terrain park of your own? Well, if you were into "getting air" as Rusty had in mind, the main ingredient needed was simply lots of snow – to pack and shape into "ramps," "tabletops," and "kickers."

A snowboard "ramp" is just what it sounds like: the snowboarder gets up to speed, goes UP a ramp – then off into the air. A "tabletop," a little more difficult to build, begins with a downslope, then the snowboarder goes across a flat table-like surface before hitting a "knuckle" -- then off into the air. A "kicker" is much like a tabletop except the surface below the incline dips down then curves back upward, like half a barrel cut from top to bottom, then laid out inside up. That curve, ending upward, provides lift.

A kicker, it should be noted, was 1) the most difficult park structure to master, and 2) provided the greatest "air" to the accomplished rider.

There was lots of lingo in the snowboarding sport. In fact, many websites tried to list and define the SO MANY terms used by insiders. Reflecting the fact of it being a relatively NEW sport, even among those who build websites on the subject, there was considerable uncertainty as to just how some of these terms were properly used.

For those who are into getting lots of air and doing tricks while aloft, perhaps the two most IMPORTANT terms were 1) a "stomp", the term for a perfect landing, versus 2) a "bailing" or "crater," when you CRASH land.

Ah, but it is only chivalrous to include one more term: "hot dog," a quality female snowboarder who tears up the slopes.

Just as in snowmobile racing, being slender and LIGHT was a big advantage in snowboarding. Perhaps Eve should consider it?

But there was more. Not only skinny and light, Rusty had

another edge, as well. Having been a local "star" in skateboarding as a teenager, Rusty was confident that he could catch on QUICKLY to snowboarding.

Well, there were lots of similarities . . .

Even though Luka had told Eve about his inoperable brain tumor and unpredictably shortened life expectancy, he did so only AFTER asking her to keep his terminal illness in confidence.

As was made clear enough to Eve by his magnanimous encouragement that she take up with someone who could offer her a future, Luka truly LOVED her. There was no doubt about that.

Still, Luka didn't realize that committing Eve to secrecy about the reason for their parting placed a heavy BURDEN on the woman he loved so dearly.

Aristotle (384 B.C. to 322 B.C.) said that human beings are "social animals." All philosophers to follow agreed, and so do does modern social science. Indeed, that's the reason that all the sciences of human behavior – from economics, to psychology, to sociology, to political science, to communication, to geography, to history – are called exactly that: the SOCIAL sciences.

Eve did UNDERSTAND Luka's reason for wanting to keep his terminal illness a secret. She realized that he prided himself on being self-reliant and didn't want people to view him as a pathetic creature; something like a crippled person.

What NEITHER of them realized was that keeping this information a secret was actually a counterproductive burden – for them BOTH.

Now, after he had effectively "pushed her away" – even from himself – each of them was walking around in essential ISOLATION with their anguish.

It was an anguish that, ironically, they were not even currently sharing with each other.

This was an intolerable situation, and something had to give.

Like Rod, Jen had decided that she, too, wanted to stay out there in "the tundra," rather than live in the city any longer. Rod was trying to drum up some business out there giving people RIDES in his hot-air balloon, and that was well and good. People would enjoy that.

Rod also had plans to draw some of his former clients – some of his frequent passengers from the city – to drive out at times to SEE the beauty of the tundra from the sky. Once again, that too, was well and good for all concerned.

Something else did not seem so well and good, however. Not to Jen. What was going on with Eve and Luka? That she had to wonder about, and she sensed something peculiar and disturbing there.

Being a newcomer to the local scene, Jen had never been close to either Eve or Luka. But, like anyone who was really GOOD at marketing, Jen was a people person. She could "read" people exceptionally well. She also had a sixth sense about social "contexts," social situations, and the situation with Eve and Luka seemed out of kilter.

Teresa knew that Rusty was up to SOMETHING out there on the snow-covered pastures of their spread. She realized that their livestock needed more attention in the winter, and especially more hay and grain to keep them warm on the inside. A "calorie," after all, is a measure of HEAT.

Teresa wasn't as FOND of those critters as Rusty seemed to be. But they did provide income sources, especially their several hundred head of cattle. The sheep and the buffalo also paid their own way. In fact, there was a BIG demand now for buffalo meat – and even more for beefalo, a cross breeding that explains itself by its name. And, shrewdly enough, Rusty had been one of the FIRST to raise and sell some of those cross-bred critters.

Fair enough. But Teresa saw no damned value in that crazy GOAT. That ornery devil seemed to thrive on just pestering the other critters out there, and to no purpose whatever.

Rusty's better half had to agree with their friends. That damned goat probably appealed to Rusty – because the two of them had so much in common.

Still, that brat of a goat was not her concern right now.

"Okay, Rusty," Teresa confronted her husband, "I saw those piles of snow. Just what in HELL are you building out there?"

Teresa was nobody's fool. Those piles of snow Rusty was spending so much time packing and shaping were NOT for the livestock.

It didn't help much that there were STARS in his eyes when Rusty answered, "It's just a little PARK; a little place for me to PLAY. Hey, Brewski likes it. He likes to ram into the ramps." (Brewski, of course, was the goat. And no one would have been surprised to learn that Rusty sometimes poured out half a beer for Brewski, his cantankerous pet, to slurp up.)

Rusty might be prone to tomfoolery, to be sure, but he didn't have an ounce of deceit in that skinny body.

He had stashed his new toy in a corner of their garage to this point, and Teresa hadn't noticed it. Now her starry-eyed husband fetched his toy and, in effect, clinched the case AGAINST himself.

"Isn't it a BEAUTY?" he asked, holding that new snowboard out for her to admire.

Admiration did not seem to be quite Teresa's frame of mind when her eyes narrowed and she blurted, "What in God's name have you brought home now?"

"It's a snowboard; kind of like a skateboard, but made for WINTER riding," Rusty reported. Then added, "Hey, it can't go very fast. It doesn't even have an engine."

"Uh huh," Teresa replied, rolling those commandingly large orbs of hers with all due SCORN.

"Didn't you break your arm on that skateboard years ago?" she now asked, in what was clearly more of an indictment than a question.

"Well, yeah. But only once. And it healed just fine," Rusty countered. "And that was before I learned how to ride it. Now, I have this stuff down pat. Besides, if I land poorly, now it will be in lots of nice, soft snow."

Rusty was clearly ready – and able – to defend his right . . . well . . . his right to be Rusty.

And that defense he was prepared to offer with an enthusiastic flair.

While Teresa just stood there slowly shaking her head . . . her face gave her away. That imp she had married was just so damned charming.

Eve and Luka were not the only ones who had dropped out of circulation. Brando seemed to have completely DISAPPEARED. At least Eve and Luka would sometimes respond to text messages, although those responses were brief and not revealing. (When anyone says, "Oh, I'm okay," they may be trying to TELL themselves that, but it's probably not accurate.)

Still, at least their friends knew that Eve and Luka were alive. Brando, on the other hand, was not responding AT ALL.

One thing was the SAME, however. Even though she had only met him once, Jen had heard quite a bit about Brando, including his WILD ideas about starting an annual Theatre Festival right there in Flathead County. More important, once again, Jen's sixth sense told her that something was seriously wrong.

"Rod, I think we should take your balloon out there where Brando is trying to build his outdoor amphitheater. If we take binoculars, maybe we can SPOT him or his vehicle -- or something – from the air."

Rod replied, "Maybe we could. But why are you so concerned about that guy? I hear he's kind of whacked."

"I'm not sure," said Jen. "I just have a strong feeling that he's out there suffering. I think something terrible has happened."

"What are you, some kind of a psychic?" Rod now asked, sincerely curious – and starting to wonder if his cute lady friend was a bit whacky herself.

But Jen's face told Rod that she didn't care what he thought of Brando, or even of her. That was not her concern right now.

Right now she expected Rod to come through – and help her find that poor man out there.

10

A Friend Loveth at all times, and a Brother is Born for Adversity (Proverbs 17:17)
(or: In the END, We only Remember those we Care for)

It was another sunny morning and the tundra was dazzling from the air.

Even with all our modern technology, there was no better way to survey ANY terrain than from the basket of a hot-air balloon. That now centuries-old conveyance provided an unimpeded and fully 360 degree view of everything below it. Yes, that view was visually breathtaking; a source of entertaining PLEASURE. It could also be of incomparable PRACTICAL value for the kind of SEARCH AND RESCUE mission upon which Jen and Rod had embarked.

Rod had given in. He had gone along with Jen's determined assertion that they should go out to survey the area where Brando was known to have been trying to build some kind of outdoor amphitheater. Never mind that most people thought Brando's project was a crackpot idea. Who was going to fill all the seats out there in that no man's land? Antelopes and coyotes?

At first, Rod had gone along with Jen's insistence on this expedition JUST to humor her. She was a cutie and a smart one, too. So he wanted to please the lady and keep in her good graces. But, even before they "lifted off" that morning, Rod, too, was now INTO the spirit of it. Didn't it say somewhere in the bible that you are your brother's keeper? (A saying roughly translated from the story of Cain and Abel. Genesis: 4:9)

Of necessity, Rod had advised Jen in ADVANCE of their search and rescue expedition . . . of a major limitation. Hot-air balloons can be steered only very VAGUELY. In fact, two of the most common answers to questions asked by passengers (or prospective passengers) as to "where we will land" are 1) "on the ground," and 2) "a hot-air balloon ride is like a Sunday afternoon drive. You don't know just where you're going, what you will see, or how long it will take."

Still, a skilled pilot can usually control the GENERAL direction of the flight – if only in a "rough estimate" kind of sense. How? By adding or releasing quantities of hot air and thereby adjusting the altitude of the flight. This does provide at least a modicum of control BECAUSE the wind normally blows in different directions at different altitudes.

The pilot will nearly always check with local airports, weather stations and/or internet sources for CURRENT wind conditions at various altitudes in ADVANCE of the flight. Normally, the pilot will – from personal experience in the area – also have his own knowledge of local altitude patterns to draw upon. In this case – as Rod was obliged to warn Jen – he had as yet VERY LITTLE experience in this particular locale.

There was one KEY upshot of this extremely limited potential for steering. Namely, on this expedition they could, AT BEST, expect to LEARN something out there. They might indeed SPOT something that would be of value in assessing Brando's situation. BUT they would NOT be able to drop down and complete a rescue mission.

If they learned something that seemed to call for an intervention, they could only RELAY that information to people equipped to DRIVE out there, perhaps in a high-profile monster truck like TMK's – or, if necessary, to those who could engage an emergency helicopter team from the county hospital.

Only the day before Rod and Jen had headed out on their expedition to find out something about Brando, Jen had made a phone call to Teresa. Like most young people, she would normally have texted Teresa. BUT IN THIS CASE she wanted to be able to

HEAR Teresa's voice – to gain some sense of Teresa's FEELINGS about the situation with Eve and Luka.

Jen realized that Teresa had known these two people FAR longer than she had.

It turned out to be a rather long call. Why? Because Teresa, too, had sensed that something was amiss there. It MIGHT be just a lovers' quarrel. But that didn't explain why neither of them wanted to talk about it. Some men don't want to talk about such things. But women nearly always DO.

TMK had decided that he needed a different vehicle. Well, actually he needed an ADDITIONAL vehicle. In short, he wasn't about to sell Daisy, his high-profile monster truck. Perish the thought. Daisy was TMK's pride and joy. But the man HAD bought a second vehicle that got better gas mileage.

Things were going well between TMK and Michelle, his demure, modest and sometimes painfully shy lady friend. Unlike Jen and Rod, however, Michelle had not decided to move out to the tundra. Well, not yet, anyway. For now, Michelle was content to stay in Kalispell, the county seat; where, in fact, she continued to live with her parents.

As happens with a man in such a circumstance, a man head over heels in love, TMK had been doing a lot of driving . . . back and forth to Kalispell on a more and more frequent basis.

So instead of his huge monster truck, TMK could now often be seen hunkered down inside his little Toyota, a tiny sport utility.

After all, amazing she was, Daisy got lousy gas mileage. That was not her job.

His friends were "ribbing" The Mighty Quinn about all of this, of course. Part of that ribbing was inspired by the fact that despite his size and well-earned bad-ass reputation, TMK was also a surprisingly SENSITIVE fellow. That, some thought, attributed to his star sign. The big brute was a Pisces. People born under that star sign are said to be likeable, empathetic, creative, kind, idealistic and – above all – highly sensitive to the reactions of other people . . . and, indeed, to everything in their immediate environments.

For that reason, his friends – although very FOND of the big fellow – couldn't resist teasing him at times. TMK would try to "laugh off" that teasing, but his face would often turn red, belying his feigned indifference to the ribbing.

A few people had suggested that their sensitivity to others (an inherent reserve and shyness) was something that TMK had in common with Michelle. Those people were correct -- and in more than one way. Not only were both of them socially sensitive, but LIKES (similarities) ATTRACT.

In point of fact, that similarity reflected WELL on TMK and Michelle's prospects for an enduring relationship. Similarities don't just attract, but the more similar prospective mates, the greater their chances of marrying, staying married, and most important, staying HAPPILY married. (R. Neff, "Loving Well: Keys to Lasting and Rewarding Relationships." 2016.)

Rusty was making good progress on his homemade snowboard "terrain park." There was just one problem: Brewski. The pet goat's fondness for ramming into things was becoming an issue. That goat was now ramming into the ramps, "table tops" and other structures that Rusty was building out there. And over and over. ALL of those structures were made entirely of snow. Even when well packed down, Brewski could do some DAMAGE by his repeated assaults.

Now, in common with many other goats – including

pets – Brewski's roaming range had been restricted by his owner. The goat was now tied to a post. The rope that limited his range was quite long, but Brewski could no longer make it to the snowboarding structures his owner was building.

Sometimes Rusty would pile up a small structure WITHIN Brewski's range; so his pet could ram into that one. Well, he liked the damned goat, you know. And he would still pour out some beer for the ornery critter once in a while.

The winds seemed to be not quite as forecast, and somewhat variable in their directions today, and Rod was struggling to guide the balloon toward where Brando was known to be working on his would-be amphitheater. It was iffy, and Rod knew that once he was passed that area, hot-air balloons were nearly impossible to turn back the other way.

But, eventually, Rod and Jen got close enough that – with the aid of their binoculars – they SPOTTED what appeared to be a TELLING sign. As nearly as they could make out, there appeared to be a vehicle at the bottom of a cliff, and it looked to be half submerged – front side down – into the snow.

Had Brando gone OFF that cliff? Was he now trapped in that half submerged vehicle?

Using their cell phones at a frantic pace, Jen and Rod were checking with Brando's friends. What kind of vehicle did he drive? What color was it?

As they feared, the vehicle they had spotted MATCHED the descriptions they were receiving of Brando's.

Soon half the phones in the county were buzzing with the news. More important, some of those phones were being used in efforts to line up one or more RESCUE missions.

The FIRST rescue squad to head out? That was Rusty and

TMK in Daisy. TMK had wanted to head out immediately, but Rusty persuaded him to wait just the few minutes it took for the county's newest snowboarder to meet up with him. And, yes, Rusty was TAKING his snowboard with them. He was also taking Brewski. Goats can go anywhere, after all. They don't call them "mountain goats" for nothing.

In just over 2 minutes, Rusty had grabbed a canteen, filled it with warm milk and strapped it to Brewski's neck.

Teresa's eyes had widened when Rusty reached for a bottle and dumped a splash of rum into the milk before he "nuked" it for 30 seconds. But Rusty had read somewhere that people used to be rescued out in the cold by rum mixed into milk. (Sure enough, the internet was FULL of such stories, dating back to as far as Lance-Corporal Cecil Withers in 1917, allegedly rescued by a Salvation Army lady who opened a tin of Carnation condensed milk and poured in some rum . . . to as recent as "Rescue," a story by Willian W. Johnstone published in 2016, albeit the last a work of fiction.)

Eve was having another bad night. It wasn't like her to be this way, she told herself. She had never been one to get upset over a silly man. There were always MORE of them out there, and she SAW how so many of them could barely disguise their carnal interest when she was in their presence.

Nor was Eve being presumptuous in that way of thinking. Nearly ALL the "Adams" she'd met were as impressed by her as that first Adam in the storied "Garden of Eden" had been. Some of them were already taken, of course. And, unfortunately, some of the others didn't have the BALLS to approach her. But they ALL wanted her.

Still, Eve admitted to herself, SHE didn't want THEM. She wanted Luka.

Eve was finally becoming ANGRY. WHY didn't that jackass call her anymore? Hey, that self-righteous bastard hadn't even texted her for over a week.

He wasn't the only man to ever be afflicted by a terminal illness, Eve told herself. It didn't give him the right to just blow her off like that – like he thought he was being some DAMNED hero in giving her up.

Eve had made up her mind. She'd had enough. It was only a little past 10:00 p.m. – not so late. She was going to call Luka. But she wasn't going to admit how angry she was. She knew that such anger in a woman wasn't very attractive to any man, and she didn't want to start a FIGHT, either.

Eve had a plan. The story of Rod and Jen's hot-air balloon sighting -- and impending plans for RESCUE efforts – was all over the local news. In truth, Eve was more interested in LUKA'S condition, than in Brando's. But this now county-wide concern over Brando gave her a good EXCUSE to call right now.

Just like Jen in her call to Teresa about the mysterious break-up, Eve didn't want to TEXT Luka. She wanted to HEAR his voice. In her case, however, that was not so much as a means to assess FEELINGS. It was more that she wanted to hear his voice as some kind of CONNECTION to him. Damn! She missed that crazy bastard.

And to HELL with his inoperable brain tumor. He wasn't dead yet.

Or was he?

By the time TMK and Rusty found their way to the cliff that

Brando had apparently gone over, there was already a medical helicopter there.

That was the good news. The bad news was that, despite their repeated efforts, that medical helicopter team had been unable to GET TO the man apparently trapped in that vehicle below the cliff.

The front half of Brando's vehicle was FIRMLY entrenched in the snow and ice.

The helicopter had packed some light cable wire – often useful in pulling vehicles out of roadside grader ditches and the like. But this time the chopper's lifting power was not ENOUGH.

As always, TMK had some of his own cables – heavier ones – on board in Daisy. And, wasting no time, he threw one of those cable lines to the helicopter crewmen still next to the half-submerged vehicle.

Those crewmen knew exactly want to do, and quickly had TMK's cable attached to the rear axle of Brando's vehicle.

Luka had NOT ANSWERED Eve's first phone call. Nor her second one. But Eve was no quitter.

If the man she loved did not answer soon, Eve would drive over and KNOCK on his door.

11

. . .CHARITY SHALL COVER THE MULTITUDE OF SINS (PETER 4:8)
(OR: LOVE IS THE ANSWER)

Christmas Day had come and gone. So had all the parties of the season. The biggest party had NOT been as wonderful as so many they had shared in years passed. Oh, there were gifts for all, and lovingly wrapped. And Teresa had done her part, with all the trimmings, goodies and activities carefully planned and provided. But Brando was still in the hospital and, although upgraded from "critical" to "serious," he was still unconscious most of the time; with only brief moments of apparent awareness and without saying anything; just looking curiously thoughtful. Some of that, the nurses reported, was probably due to all the painkillers he was receiving for his frostbite and internal injuries.

In brief, Brando was alive . . . for now. Whether he would pull through, and, if he did, what kind of condition his body – and his brain – would ultimately retain . . . was still MUCH IN DOUBT.

Luka and Eve had attended that "always the biggest Christmas party" at Rusty and Teresa's; and they had come TOGETHER, to most everyone's relief. But they were both subdued and quiet; just sitting together, looking like they were lost in their own thoughts most of the time. Indeed, on more than one occasion, another guest had said something like, "Excuse me, Luka (or Eve) . . . did you HEAR what I just said?"

The liveliest part of the gathering came at TMK's expense, when he was repeatedly teased about his little Toyota, with lines like, "Don't you feel guilty making that little thing haul YOUR huge carcass around?" Or: "Who weighs more, T. M? You or that CUTE little foreign job you're driving now?" Then, predictably enough, the same smart aleck would add, "Just Kidding, T.M. We know Daisy DESERVES some rest after SAVING Brando," or some other "backhanded compliment" or acknowledgment of TMK's typically broad-shouldered response to the emergency.

In fact, they were all quite proud of The Mighty Quinn, and in admiration of the heroic reputation he so rightly deserved. Yet, they HAD to tease him a little, too, including about Michelle. "She's so pretty and refined. What's she doing with you? . . . Oh, it must be Beauty and the Beast," was a typical quip on that score. But Rusty's offering was perhaps the prize-winner here: "Don't worry, Big Fella. We'll take up a collection to send you to CHARM SCHOOL."

In keeping with Luka's wishes, Eve had kept his medical condition a secret. But at least the two of THEM were talking again, and Eve was trying to take the proverbial "bull by the horns," and sometimes sharing her thoughts on that otherwise banned subject.

Once again, Eve was no quitter. She had decided that there MUST be SOMETHING they could do. First of all, she was suggesting that Luka should get a SECOND OPINION. Luka, having resigned himself to his fate, was not receptive to that idea. It seemed that he didn't want to get his hopes up; only to have to, later, go through the whole painful process of "letting go" of his hopes again.

Nevertheless, Eve would persist. "Luka, it is only LOGICAL to get a second opinion." And her suggestion was rapidly morphing into a more and more INSISTENT opinion, one that Luka could not ignore.

"I know you love me, Luka. And if you love me, you should do it FOR ME." Soon Luka was starting to relent. "If that's what you really want, Eve," he finally said, and a little smile came to his face with that concession.

Even if he WAS dying, it was good to be loved.

Although not attuned to his surroundings now, there was a lot going on INSIDE of Brando's head. He was thinking about Stacy – and all the things she had told him.

Stacy was a Native American, a member of the Salish-speaking tribes, collectively known as "Flatheads," despite the fact that the people now known by that name had never engaged in the bizarre head flattening that anthropologists loved to write about. And that was just the tip of a GIANT iceberg of LIES told by the Pilgrims about her people.

Brando had discovered Stacy when she was skillfully piloting a canoe down one of the MANY fast-running and rock-infested mountain streams out in the wilds of the Western Montana "tundra." He had STOOD on one bank of that whitewater river admiring Stacy, almost in love at first sight of his "Indian Princess."

Although Brando thought of Stacy as an "Indian Princess" (that in keeping with his bent for the theatrical), she was actually not at home in either the traditional culture of her forbears NOR in what she called the "Pilgrim" world.

Brando was not at home in any world either, and that was true enough even BEFORE his accident and resultant coma.

Yes, Brando and Stacy had something in common.

Brewski, Rusty's pet goat, could no longer make his way to the ramps, "table tops" and other snow-boarding structures the county's favorite dare devil was building out there on he and Teresa's spread. But another critter HAD made it there. It was a Golden Eagle.

Unlike the goat, this critter was not there to ram or otherwise do damage to those structures, but just as Rusty himself, to PLAY on them. Rusty was surprised to see his feathered visitor repeatedly coming in from the air, to SLIDE down, then up, then OFF back into the air – just like an accomplished snowboarder getting "air" with all due finesse.

All of this the giant bird did with its prodigiously large wings widely spread, providing not only a delightful show, but a commanding presence.

Golden Eagles abound in Western Montana. About the same size as America's official Emblem, the Bald Eagle, both species of giant birds are native to Flathead County. Both birds are highly intelligent, but what strikes one first is their SIZE. Both are about three feet long, weighing roughly 10-12 pounds as adults. When on the ground -- where you can sometimes see them close up -- their wingspans of over 6 feet can be truly breathtaking.

Rusty had an idea. What if he trained a Bald Eagle to do tricks like that? He could become famous.

Hey, that wasn't such a crazy idea. After all, The Bald Eagle was selected VERY EARLY by our revolutionary forefathers, on June 20, 1782 as the official emblem of the United States. Why? Because of its long life, great strength and majestic looks. Further, at that time, it was also believed to exist only on this continent.

That choice was NOT universally acclaimed at the time. Ben Franklin wrote:

> "I wish that the bald eagle had not been chosen as
> the representative of our country, he is a bird of bad
> moral character, he does not get his living honestly,
> you may have seen him perched on some dead tree,
> where, too lazy to fish for himself, he watches the
> labor of the fishing-hawk, and when that diligent
> bird has at length taken a fish, and is bearing it to
> its nest for the support of his mate and young ones,
> the bald eagle pursues him and takes it from him....
> Besides he is a rank coward; the little kingbird, not

bigger than a sparrow attacks him boldly and drives him out of the district. He is therefore by no means a proper emblem for the brave and honest . . . of America . . . . For a truth, the turkey is in comparison a much more respectable bird, and withal a true original native of America . . . a bird of courage, and would not hesitate to attack a grenadier of the British guards, who should presume to invade his farmyard with a red coat on."

(https://www.baldeagleinfo.com/eagle/eagle9.html)

(Ben Franklin was a truly important, brilliant and courageous American patriot, but between the reader and myself, I would not vote for the Turkey. As I farm boy, I learned that those birds, however tasty on the Thanksgiving table, are flatly stupid -- making the lowly chicken look like a genius by comparison. I would vote to stick with the Bald Eagle, the smart bird.)

As Rusty approached, the Golden Eagle eyed him, did another performance on Rusty's snowboard structures, and then hung in the air OVER him for several minutes.

Rusty was not afraid. Neither was the bird. Instead, it seemed . . . well, like a small meeting of a mutual admiration society.

Michelle was, ever so slowly, starting to tell The Mighty Quinn things that he wasn't prepared for. As per her own lips, Michelle's childhood had been – as she recalled it in painful flashbacks – both a HELL and a TRIAL. The "hell" was the not so unusual reality of a child living in the home of a raging alcoholic. "Raging,"

to be sure, was neither an overstatement nor a metaphor. The "trial" was trying to hang in there -- and protect her mother, as best she could.

Now TMK was coming to understand WHY Michelle was still living with her parents.

"I'll kill him," TMK said. But Michelle, her body now trembling, replied, "No. Then you'll go to jail and I'll lose you."

Some things could not be solved by BRUTE strength alone, as The Mighty Quinn had learned before. Instead, it took patience. And Michelle was a TOWER of patience. That too, TMK was coming to learn.

Like most people who had attended Rusty and Teresa's "always the biggest Christmas party," Jen was somewhat relieved to see that Luka and Eve had both made it, and that they had come together. Even more than the others there, however, Jen was ACUTELY aware that they were both oddly quiet, and seemed to be worried about something.

Walking over and waiting until she was sure that Luka was finally making eye contact with her, Jen asked, "How is business at the shop, Luka?" Jen, only newly moved to the tundra, had never visited Barron's Plumbing, Heating, TV, Appliance & Electronics, the family business that Luka had been obliged to take over after his father's injury. So Luka was a bit surprised at that question. He was not suspicious, however, because – as the ONLY local store and repair shop for so many different products and services -- EVERYONE in the entire county knew about that business.

Assuming that Jen was just wanting to be friendly, Luka gave his standard answer, "Business is almost TOO good. But I guess that's better than the alternative."

"No doubt," agreed Jen, with what she intended as a properly bemused smile, in appreciation of Luka's artful line. "And how is the family?" she continued.

While Jen could not be expected to know much if anything about his family, that, too, was no surprise – but just a STANDARD inquiry in a rural area, almost a polite formality. So was Luka's answer: "Oh, everyone is fine. So far."

But Jen was FISHING. She was pretty sure that SOMETHING wasn't fine. So now she turned to Eve, "Any snowmobile races coming up, Eve?"

Unlike Luka, Eve WAS becoming a little suspicious. Besides, Eve hadn't forgotten that Jen had "stolen" her boyfriend back in Middle School, and she'd better NOT be trying to make inroads with Luka.

Rolling her eyes in an age-old gesture, sometimes involuntary and sometimes quite contrived (it was always difficult to tell) of irritation or annoyance, Eve curtly replied, "Maybe. But that's my own business."

Now Luka glanced at Eve, then back at Jen. He had to WONDER just what that was all about. But not really UP for talking about it, he just turned his attention back to the drink in his hand.

Jen's effort to turn up a clue as to what was TROUBLING Luka and Eve was getting no traction at all, as she quickly realized. And she just excused herself with "I'd better go see if Teresa needs any help in the kitchen. I don't know how she manages to DO all this."

Brando was surprised to learn that Stacy didn't really feel comfortable with her fellow Salish-speaking natives on the reservation. But at least part of the reason for that was clear enough. Stacy's tribe – like so many others – had started "taking the Pilgrim's road," especially with the crass and greedy rush to open all those "gaming centers," as they called them; those gambling casinos. Along with that, they had started fighting among themselves – and even trying to DENY some of their relatives, disputing their bloodlines. Why? So they could keep MORE of the "gaming proceeds" for themselves.

On the other hand, Stacy was very much committed to her own FAMILY – her brothers and sisters. Like her, they received quarterly "gaming payments," but they HAD'NT bought into trying to erect barriers – trying to DENY shares to other relatives.

In truth, Stacy thought the whole gaming thing – all that MONEY – was a scourge on her people. It was a scourge they had brought on themselves by taking the Pilgrim's road.

Like many Native Americans at this point – Stacy saw herself as having more in common with the creatures of the wild than with her human peers. And her friends and family had both noticed and commented on that, even when she was still a child.

Also like many Native Americans today – especially those born on a reservation – Stacy had two different names. One was a Pilgrim-sounding name that had been put on their birth certificate, and the name they normally used in interacting with outsiders. They also had a name that was in their own tongue, and was not necessarily intended to be written down. After all, their traditional cultures were not of books or writing, but were "oral" traditions.

Stacy's traditional name, the one in her own native tongue, meant "Stands like a Bear." In English, its sound would be written roughly, "Witata Kata."

In some Native American tribes – including Stacy's – that native name would be given quite a while AFTER the child's birth, when the person had shown a particular personal trait. And, yes, it could certainly be said that Stacy stood like a bear. She looked like she was firmly anchored to the ground with each step -- and was not one to be trifled with.

In the Pilgrim vernacular, Stacy had "sass."

They were about to learn that at the hospital -- where Brando was still "in recovery."

12

TO EVERY THING THERE IS A SEASON . . . (ECCLESIASTES 3:1)
(OR: TIME MAY YET A PATH REVEAL)

It was a small party, just two couples, Rod and Jen; TMK and Michelle.

It was Jen's idea to invite TMK and Michelle to join them for the evening. That idea had come to Jen after what her cousin TMK had shared with her.

Jen was not surprised at what TMK had told her about Michelle's childhood and continued concern for her mother. In earning her A.S. degree in Marketing, Jen had been required to take a psychology course. Finding that she liked that course, she had taken a second one, Introduction to Clinical Psychology, as an elective. While her A.S. in Marketing was only a 2-year degree, Jen had gone on to take other courses beyond her requirements, ending up with nearly enough credits to earn a B.S. or B.A. degree. Maybe she would go back and complete a 4-year degree at some point.

One of the extra college courses Jen had taken was Introduction to Social Work. In conjunction with the Clinical Psychology elective, that social work course had taught Jen that childhoods like Michelle's were actually quite common. Worse perhaps, those problematic childhoods often resulted in lifelong personality problems, including emotional disorders.

As adults, children from such backgrounds typically had trust issues. The GOOD news was that most such victims responded WELL to just being SLOWLY befriended by people who were warmhearted and accepting of them, despite their shyness. A SMALL group was much more comfortable to them than a larger one, but that was not so strange, was it? Most people were more comfortable in small groups than in large crowds.

Before inviting them to the little party, Jen had reassured TMK that Michelle's childhood was not so unusual, and that all she needed was for people to go SLOW in getting to know her.

Otherwise, ALL of us are, as Aristotle put it, "social animals." We don't do well in isolation.

Well, it had to happen. Rusty had succeeded not only in building his own snowboarding "terrain park," and in proving – at least to his own satisfaction – that it was basically the same as the skateboarding he had mastered as a teen, he was now entered in a snowboarding CONTEST to see who could get the most "air" (the highest lift) while jumping over Canyon Creek.

Located near the North Fork of the Flathead River, the Canyon Creek trail system was designed primarily for SNOWMOBILES. But now it was marked off on special occasions for snowboarding contests. Most of those entering would be satisfied just to stay on the over 80 miles of marked and groomed trails of the Flathead National Forest. But a few would want to try for the "big air" – jumping OVER the creek after which the park was named.

Hey, that Golden Eagle had been quite IMPRESSIVE -- showing his stuff with all due finesse out in Rusty's private terrain park. But that big bird had nothing on Rusty, still the county's favorite dare devil.

Thanks to Eve, Luka now had an appointment to get a second opinion. That appointment was at St. Peter's Health, the largest hospital in Montana. St. Peter's was 3 hours and 22 minutes away -- in Helena, the state capital.

At this point, Eve was not messing around. After talking to half a dozen receptionists and nurses at local clinics and doctors' offices, Luka's woman had decided that the doctors there were all AFRAID of giving a second opinion.

Eve wasn't sure why. Were they all afraid of a possible medical malpractice suit? Or was medicine in America today just one big CLUB – where STICKING together and protecting their rights to charge MASSIVE fees was a case of money over medicine?

Either way, Eve expected that St. Peter's, largely funded by moneys from the Catholic Church, would be independent of that malice and/or self-serving greed.

And there WAS – or at least appeared to be – evidence on that side. Everyone in Flathead County knew of SOMEONE who had been SAVED by the mercy of doctors at St. Peter's Health, the hospital in Helena.

Because of their reputation – and hence the large numbers of souls who SOUGHT help there – St. Peter's always had a backlog of prospective patients waiting to be seen. Unless your case was immediately life-threatening, you could expect to wait a month or more to be admitted.

That waiting list now included Luka.

The scene at the County Hospital in Kalispell was a bit different.

Stacy, A.K.A. "Stands like a Bear," was determined to break Brando OUT of their admitted numbers. She knew old Native American cures for frostbite and nearly frozen internal organs -- and trusted that traditional medicine MORE than the Pilgrim's.

Maybe Brando's "Indian Princess" had connections with the local spirits (don't rule that one out), or maybe not. But, for whatever reason, upon hearing her voice in the hallway – even BEFORE she marched right passed the attendants trying to tell her that Brando couldn't see visitors now – he was suddenly conscious and wide awake when she BURST into his room.

Brando's eyes said it all. Somehow he had KNOWN that she

would come. His princess then CONFIRMED his faith – and more.

To the doctor and two attendants who had quickly followed her into his room, Stacy announced, "He's awake. And he has rights."

Turning now to Brando himself, his princess asked, "What do YOU want to do, my brave warrior?"

As only Brando could, he rose from that bed – and waving one arm outward with a theatrical flair not bested by any actor before him, declared, "This is my lady, my angel, my life . . . . She will CARE for me now . . . and we will be taking our LEAVE this hour."

Luka had found that just going about his normal ways – his old routines – was "good medicine." No, he was not thinking about it like a Native American "medicine man;" he wasn't Native American, not even in part, so far as he knew. He was just finding that continuing his daily routines -- rising at the same time as he had for years now, and heading to his shop – was what WORKED for him.

Was it strange? Luka was also finding that making his customers happy – whether with repairs or promising to deliver the EXACT same appliance they had found on the internet (but with his own service guarantee added) STILL provided him the same sense of satisfaction as always. No one lives forever, he was now thinking. We just do what we can, WHILE we can.

Somehow, it didn't seem to matter now . . . that with his brain tumor, his life could end at any moment.

At times Luka even TRIED to share this inner peace he had found – his being "ok" with a shortened life – with Eve.

Upon hearing this, the WONDER of Luka's life would smile and touch his face in a gesture of enduring appreciation for the man, but that was ONLY what her HEART had to say. Her MIND was not having that story.

By now, Eve had contacted every top-flight medical center in the nation – including 3 Mayo Clinics. Someone, somewhere, somehow, could SAVE her chosen Adam. Eve had no doubt of that.

Just like St. Peters Health, the state's leading hospital in Helena, ALL of these top-flight medical centers had long waiting lists. Only patients in critical condition could be seen right away; nearly always brought in from other medical facilities by ambulance.

But Eve believed in an old saying tracing back to the days of covered wagons: "The squeaky wheel gets the grease." And she had kept calling St. Peter's every few days – to check Luka's place on their waiting list.

Luka FINALLY had an appointment scheduled with a brain surgeon, Eve had just learned. It was three and a half weeks off, but she intended to KEEP calling. An earlier appointment was possible, as others waiting would sometimes go elsewhere, appear to spontaneously recover – or, yes, DIE waiting.

Maybe they were shocking, even UNNATURAL. Yes, maybe the things Jen was thinking of doing to Rod's body were . . . well, a little INCEST would likely raise fewer eyebrows.

But it was ALL Rod's fault; what with him running off . . . halfway across the country. Boston? Perhaps the song said it best,

You spend an awful lot of time in Massachusetts . . .
You say that it's important for our future . . .
Each time duty calls you got to give it all . . .
I packed your bags and left them in the hallway

But before you leave again there's just one thing
you outta know
When the icy winds blow through you remember that it's
me
Who feels the cold most of all

(Lines from "Whoever's in New England." By Reba McIntire. Released 1986.)

Rod CLAIMED that his trips to Boston were all BUSINESS. There was supposed to be an old and influential hot-air balloon "society" back there, with elite ancestry tracing back to the "Boston Blue Bloods." Good connections there could yield some lucrative business, "well-heeled" customers from all across the country ready to pay the big bucks -- to see the amazing Montana tundra from that old-fashioned and still unrivaled aerial vantage point.

Well, maybe. But Jen was suspicious. She could appreciate that Rod wanted to be a big success, and was truly devoted to trying to achieve that success within his CHOSEN field of hot-air ballooning.

But her intuition told her there was some WOMAN back there.

The next time Rod returned, Jen planned to IMPRESS him with some creative erotic tricks . . . tricks she'd bet that Boston prude had never imagined to exist.

In a word, Jen intended to be unforgettable.

For their part, the staff at the county hospital had been impressed by Brando's energy and DRAMATIC (he could do no otherwise) display of recovery.

Indeed, Brando also REFUSED to get back into that bed, and proceeded to disconnect himself from the intravenous feeding tube that had been stuck in one of his arms for days – and, of course, with a flourish, complete with facial gestures deliberately revealing his casual and self-amused defiance.

The staff DID manage to persuade Brando that they needed to check his vital signs. But the results of those tests were equally as impressive as his theatrical flair.

Just as he had proclaimed, Stacy and Brando would take leave of that county hospital within the hour of Stacy's bold arrival.

Rusty was practicing up for the contest – his planned attempt to get "the biggest air" in a snowboarding jump over Canyon Creek. Unfortunately, Teresa was becoming suspicious. Unlike Jen, Teresa was NOT suspicious that her man was cheating on her. She suspected that he was up to something CRAZY.

Now . . . where would Teresa get an idea like that?

Rusty hadn't said a thing to her – or to any of their friends – about "The Great Canyon Creek Leap," as it was now being billed. So why would she suspect anything like that from the county's favorite dare devil?

For a while, it seemed like Luka's dizzy spells had largely gone away. Then, WHAM, they had come back – and worse than ever. Now Luka was doing those Brandt-Daroff exercises his doctor had prescribed to relieve the dizziness EVERY morning. Sometimes he had to do those exercises OVER AND OVER . . . before he felt stable enough to go to work.

Eve had started dropping into Luka's shop almost every work day now. Was she checking up on him? Was she being something of a mother hen?

Luka had little doubt that Eve was doing exactly that. But he had come to realize that such LOVE was nothing to belittle. Indeed, it was a WONDER to appreciate. And he would smile and be ready to hug and kiss her when she dropped in; so long as his hands weren't covered with grime from some repair in progress.

Today, however, Eve would find that the shop was not open. That was odd. It was a little past 9:30 A.M., and Luka had always opened at 8:00 A.M. sharp.

The fact was that Luka hadn't been able to get his dizziness under control that morning . . . at least, not yet.

13

AND I SAW A NEW HEAVEN . . . (REVELATION 21:1)
(OR: THERE ARE MORE THINGS IN HEAVEN AND EARTH . . . THAN DREAMT OF {SHAKESPEARE: HAMLET})

Luka had to wonder if it was real, or just in his mind. Shortly after Eve FINALLY decided to go on home – satisfied that he wasn't dying yet – there was a knocking at his door.

It was a strange time for anyone to knock on his door – now nearing midnight.

Luka had been "bluffing" a little – trying his BEST to reassure Eve. The truth was that, without expending great effort, Luka was having trouble TELLING reality from the hallucinations that would now INVADE his mind at this time of night.

> While I nodded, nearly napping, suddenly there came a tapping,
> As of someone gently rapping, rapping at my chamber door.
> "Tis some visitor," I muttered, "tapping at my chamber door --
> Only this and nothing more." . . . .
>
> Presently my soul grew stronger; hesitating then no longer,
> "Sir," said I, "or Madam, truly your forgiveness I implore . . . .
> Here I opened wide the door --
> Darkness there and nothing more.
>
> (Lines from "The Raven." By Edgar Allan Poe. First published in 1845.)

It had been a long day. Upon finding it oddly closed, Eve had gone straight from Luka's shop to his apartment that day. By the time she arrived, he was FINALLY getting his dizziness under control – and ready to go to work.

Eve was skeptical. "Maybe you should just take the day off," she implored him. "Give your body some time to rest. You probably

NEED that." Luka had smiled and hugged her. And – what the hell – why not? She might be right.

After all, Eve was a nurse. She was an LPN and nearing completion of her coursework for an RN degree.

In any case, Luka wanted to show Eve the RESPECT his loving woman so richly deserved -- as well as do his best to EASE her mind a bit.

So the shop remained closed that day.

Eve had gone back to work at the county hospital in Kalispell. Yes, that was the same hospital from which Brando, at Stacy's bold instigation, had recently made his escape; although Eve had not been on duty at that time.

Traffic was NOT an issue in rural Montana, and it was only a 20-minute drive from Luka's place to the hospital.

On her lunch break, Eve had returned to check up on Luka.

When she arrived, he was in the midst of a round of his Brandt-Daroff exercises. He hadn't experienced a relapse into dizzy spells, but his doctor had emphasized that it was a good idea to DO these exercises as often as possible. They could have a PREVENTIVE value.

Eve was starting to realize that Luka, her treasured Adam, had a "philosophical" side to him. Given a chance, he was always prone to find an UP side to any situation.

Maybe that was one reason she was SO taken with the big lug.

In this case, Luka was again suggesting to Eve that just following out his routines gave him a sense of inner peace. By now, those Brandt-Daroff exercises had become a part of his life rituals. So NOW doing those exercises was DOUBLY beneficial. They didn't just ward off dizzy spells, but also added to his sense of contentment and satisfaction with life, despite its current challenges and tribulations.

"I think you are becoming something like a Buddhist Monk,"

Eve said. That was neither a compliment nor a criticism on her part. But just an observation. And that observation was astute. At this point, Luka's view of life had much in common with the "stoic" thinking of The Buddha. (Although his exact dates of birth and death are not clear, this thinker was born sometime prior to 445 B.C. in Ancient India. Also regarded as a philosopher, Gautama Buddha is now recognized as the founder of the world religion of Buddhism.)

"Not quite," Luka replied. "Those monks swear off sexual pleasure. I'm not going there." Then with a devilish look in his eyes, Eve's chosen hunk of a man added, "We're ALREADY in my bed. Is this a good time?"

In point of fact, it was on his bed that – as per instructions – Luka always did his Brandt-Daroff exercises. And that bed could be put to more interesting use.

Yes, it had been a long day – and, while challenging at times, Luka had found it both satisfying and even memorable. So long as he shall live, he would remember every embrace, tease, titillation and delicious release of pent-up passion he had shared with Eve that day.

But now it was midnight. And just what WAS that knocking at his door.

Finally getting up and going to the door, at first there appeared to be NO ONE there at all. Hmmm . . . Maybe the person knocking had given up and gone away. Or maybe, as Luka had suspected, it was just a hallucination. His mind might be at peace, but that tumor in his brain seemed to be playing tricks on him at times . . . especially late at night, when he was nearing sleep.

Then it came swooping passed him, and circled back. It was

a snow white dove . . . finally dropping a small, but lushly green olive branch at Luka's feet.

The symbolism was amazing. Whether that dove was real or just a product of his imagination, Luka saw this delivery as SIGN of something powerful and hopeful.

For centuries the expression "to extend an olive branch" had meant to offer peace or reconciliation, an end to a conflict. Its origin traced to the book of Genesis -- when Noah sent out a dove, who returned with an olive branch. That, of course, was a sign that the biblical flood was over, that God had ended his wrathful deluge.

Although there were several varieties of doves found in Montana, a SNOW WHITE one was RARE. On the other hand, olive trees, especially a variety known as Russian olive trees were plentiful. Not native to the state, they were introduced in the 1930s in the hope of saving the soil amidst the widespread drought that had claimed much of the American Midwest and West as a "Dust Bowl." Now, because they were almost TOO plentiful, whether those trees were seen as a boon or PEST depended on who you asked.

But issues of ecology were not on Luka's mind here. He saw that dove and its delivery as an omen. It was almost enough to bring the man to a religious epiphany, to make him a believer.

> When Noah had drifted
> on the flood many days
> He searched for land (He searched for land)
> In various ways (various ways) . . .
>
> On the wings of a snow-white dove
> He sends His pure sweet love
> A sign from above (sign from above)
> On the wings of a dove (wings of a dove)

(Lines from "Wings of A Snow White Dove." First released by Ferlin Husky in 1960)

The next day Luka made it to work on time, and opened the shop door for business at 8:00 A.M. sharp. He didn't feel dizzy and was happy to chat with the occasional customer who dropped in – whether they had come to do business or just to pass the time. That's the way it was in rural Montana, and Luka was fine with that.

At this point, Luka didn't know whether that dove – and its olive branch – were REAL or just a hallucination. But that, too, was fine – and either way.

The most important thing was that the love of his life, Eve, was standing BY him through all of this.

Luka, like his father and HIS father before him, was a baseball fan. There were no Major League baseball teams in Montana, nor anywhere close to them. So fans there just CHOSE any team that suited their dreams. (There was a hit move about baseball called "The Field of Dreams," starring Kevin Costner and released in 1989. That movie's title aptly summed up so much about what baseball MEANT to its fans.)

Luka's father was a Los Angeles Dodgers fan. Mighty fine to that! The Brooklyn and then L.A. Dodgers had a RICH tradition . . . all the way back to Duke Snyder and Sandy Koufax.

And baseball was ALL about tradition. What team had even MORE tradition behind it than the Dodgers? That would be Luka's team, the New York Yankees. There would never be another Babe Ruth. That audacious scalawag – who grew up in an orphanage – hit 60 home runs in one year, and this was when most TEAMS in the majors didn't send that many balls "out of the park" in a season.

Now almost no one remembered that "The Babe" had ALSO been a PITCHER in the Major Leagues. And one of the very best.

He never pitched for The Yankees. He had done that with the Red Sox.

That pitching by Babe Ruth was not only Major League quality – but, along with the Bambino's more storied bat, helped The Boston Red Sox win THREE World Series titles in just 6 years.

Despite all of that, Babe Ruth would then be traded to another team. Why? For money. Big money.

Harry Herbert Frazee (1881-1929), owner of The Red Sox at the time, had other aspirations beyond baseball titles. He was ALSO trying to make it big on Broadway. Harry thought he had a blockbuster – in a play called, "No, No, Nanette." He intended to FINANCE that play with the money The New York Yankees paid him for "The Babe."

The rest is history – a history called "The Curse of The Bambino." The Red Sox would not win another World Series for 86 years – from 1918 until 2004.

Meanwhile, the Yankees, until then not much at all -- with The Babe on their roster – suddenly became the dominant team in the majors.

Before acquiring Babe Ruth, The New York Yankees didn't even have a stadium. They had played on a multipurpose open-air field called "The Meadowlands" – a humble venue with little seating. Soon they would enjoy the ever-so-impressive venue of Yankee Stadium, rightly called "The House that Ruth Built."

And that was only the beginning of pin stripe tradition. From there, the Yankees would go on to win 27 World Series championships. Still the most by ANY team – and by a WIDE margin.

What is the second most World Series titles won by a team? That would be eleven (11). And what team holds that claim to second? Well, it isn't the Red Sox . . . but the St. Louis Cardinals

Yes, just like his father, Luka was a baseball fan, and he agreed with what his father always said: "The BEST thing about SPORTS is that they don't really matter. They just provide an escape from life's troubles."

At this point, Luka's father did not get out much. After his accident, he couldn't even walk. But he was still a lucky man – and he knew it. His wife, Luka's mother, had stood by him. And STILL did.

It seemed to be a tradition in the family to give sons UNUSUAL names. "Something to live up to," his grandmother said. And Luka's father had been named "Reginald." Now "Reggie" (as he loved to be called . . . in appreciation of Reggie Jackson, a famous Power Hitter – even if he WAS a Yankee rather than a Dodger) mostly just watched T.V. But – by subscription – Reggie could watch nearly EVERY Major League Baseball game.

Luka's father also subscribed to channels bringing in professional baseball games from Japan, Korea, Puerto Rico . . . and elsewhere . . . year around.

On the subject of The New York Yankees and baseball tradition, it would be remiss not to mention Lou Gehrig, a figure much larger than the game itself.

While still in his prime, Gehrig had contracted ALS

(Amyotrophic lateral sclerosis), which even today remains a devastating diagnosis; and of course, is still widely called, "Lou Gehrig disease."

Fittingly for an American hero, it was the Fourth of July; specifically July 4, 1939. Over 61,000 fans were packed into what was already being called "the House that Ruth Built."

But they were NOT there that day to celebrate the Bambino. They had come to witness Lou Gehrig's early retirement, and what would become one of the most widely quoted speeches of all time.

Because of his immense popularity, and radio broadcasts, the audience to Gehrig's speech was by no means limited to the thousands of fans present, but also heard by MILLIONS across America.

Falling squarely into the category of reality being stranger than fiction, the man whose muscles had suddenly become depleted, had -- until THEN -- been known as "The Iron Horse," having played 2,130 consecutive games, with never a game off for injury or illness.

And now that same man had taken himself out of the game, realizing that he must retire early due to his physical inability to compete.

But it was what Lou Gehrig SAID that was the most surprising and inspiring thing of all. Despite his diagnosis, and a very poor prognosis, the man proclaimed, "Today I consider myself the luckiest man on the face of the earth."

Because of Eve, so did Luka.

14

. . .THEN SHALL ALL THE TREES OF THE WOOD REJOICE (PSALM 96:12)
(OR: YOU ARE PART OF NATURE. EMBRACE IT)

With Michelle at his side, Cory, a.k.a. "The Mighty Quinn," a.k.a. "T.M.," a.k.a. "TMK," had just exited I-90. Turning sharply north onto Route 93, they were beginning to climb.

About seven miles up that STEEP roadway that had somehow been carved by human effort along the mountain's edge -- and now about 4,000 feet higher -- they arrived at Evaro, marking the southern boundary of the Flathead Indian Reservation.

It was late January -- dead into the winter -- and this was NOT a route MOST vehicles should take at this time of year. But Michelle and TMK were in Daisy, his high-rise monster truck, and Daisy could go most ANYWHERE at any time.

For her part, Michelle was feeling perfectly comfortable alongside The Mighty Quinn, even though she could SEE quite clearly that should they go OFF the edge of that Mountainside roadway, it would be a LONG fall. "You DO like to take things big, don't you, T.M.?" his normally timid lady asked -- now with evident confidence and admiration in her voice.

"I guess you could say that," her chosen hero answered, with that CHEESY grin for which he was well known.

Indeed, there was no point in trying to deny it. TMK wasn't just large in stature, he relished "big productions." And, as his friends could attest, he usually pulled them off well.

It wasn't February just yet, but Michelle would soon learn . . . occasion by occasion . . . that TMK had one birthday party the FIRST week of February, another the SECOND week, and so on. And people in his circle would come to them ALL.

If someone NEW to the circle would say, "Wait, I thought Cory's birthday was LAST week," or something along that line, TMK would eventually allow, "Hey, it's like Black History Month," and everyone would laugh -- almost as heartily as TMK himself. (Never mind that February WAS black History month, and that TMK may or may not have known that -- it was just an EXCUSE to take it big, as he always did. It was just for the FUN of it.)

But there was more to this outing than Cory taking it big. The SCENERY was awe-inspiring. Montana is known as "Big Sky" country, but especially in the state's northwest reaches, the landscape looms every bit as large.

In a word, they were enjoying nature's SPLENDOR. It was nature at her best -- some of her breathtaking natural wonders.

And it was good for their souls.

Many people would look around at their world and say, "I don't think I belong here." And they may be right.

Sometimes one needs to keep searching -- to FIND what feels like home. But not TMK. He was MADE for Montana.

Just like Luka and his father, TMK was a lucky man.

As she had known almost from the moment of meeting The Mighty Quinn, it could equally be said that Michelle was a lucky woman.

Rusty, too, had always been a lucky devil. And if we may DARE to mix cheeky satanic tomfooleries here, this overly intrepid HELLION of the daring variety probably NEEDED all of his luck -- and maybe more.

But not this time. After doing a little research on the internet, Teresa had figured it out. ALL that time Rusty had been spending out there in their pasture, building those ramps and other hardened snow structures, was NOT for the livestock. It was for some more of her crazy husband's high jinks.

"Rusty, what do you know about this 'Great Canyon Creek Leap' that is now being promoted right down the road from us?" Rusty just smiled with that baby-faced grin that had served him so well on so many occasions.

But Teresa was not having it. "I'm waiting for your answer," she said, with those commandingly big blue eyes of hers now making clear that she had seen through this caper -- and was not about to let him off the hook.

"Oh, Sweet Baby Cakes, it isn't really a canyon. It's only a creek. They just NAMED it Canyon creek."

"Uh Huh," Teresa deadpanned, with those prominent blue eyes still sending the same message. "And WHY did they name it CANYON creek, Rusty?"

"Well, I guess it IS kind of a deep creek. But it isn't very WIDE. I can clear that little creek EASY. I'll be just fine."

Teresa's eyes were telling another story. Rusty would be just fine, because he was NOT going to leap over that creek.

Another fellow in the neighborhood (well, when he was home) WASN'T so lucky. It just might be that HIS luck had run out.

Jen had changed her mind. When Rod got back from New England, she wouldn't try to impress him with creative erotic tricks. She would SAVE those -- for someone who DESERVED them.

As for Rod, he would get the cold shoulder when he got back this time. Or maybe he'd get no shoulder at all -- not from Jen, at least.

Jen-Jen was on the hunt . . . for a new man.

Where was that guy they called "Brando?"

She had only met him a couple of times, both at parities where she was with Rod and hadn't had a chance to get to know him. But that guy did have a swagger about him. To Jen, as indeed to many others, Brando seemed to move like a big cat. There were some fine muscles at work there. Any woman could see that.

Yes, she had heard that Brando was half crazy. Building a

huge outdoor amphitheater in the middle of nowhere? And telling people he expected to start an annual theater FESTIVAL there, just like the world-famous FILM festival held yearly in their sister state of Utah?

Ok, that was quite a stretch. The Sundance Film Festival in Utah was started and continued to be promoted by Robert Redford – one of the most famous actors in America. Whereas, despite his own theatrical flair, to most of the world . . . Brando was a nobody.

And maybe he was just wacky.

But everyone knew that some of the greatest artists and creative thinkers of all time -- from famous writers like Tolstoy and Poe, to Picasso and Van Gogh with their paint brushes -- were probably a little off their nuts. And sometimes they DID exactly what they set out to do, despite all the reservations and doubts about their sanity.

Who would know how to drop a hint to Brando -- a hint that she might be interested in him? That would be Teresa, thought Jen.

When he was not out there working on his ambitious project -- that outdoor amphitheater in the midst of nowhere -- Brando was an insurance agent. Actually, he was the owner of his own insurance agency.

That insurance agency had been founded by his grandfather.

Brando's grandfather was one shrewd dude. Somewhat like his grandson, he also had BIG aspirations. When Brando was still in elementary school, his grandfather had confided some INSIDE information to him: Selling insurance is one of the few ways that the average man (or woman) can "make a killing," becoming financially well off.

If you are building your own agency from scratch, you will

have to work hard for many years when you are a young man or woman -- making lots of "cold" contacts.

BUT if you are likable, outgoing, and always take care of your customers well, by the time you reach middle age, it becomes an easy job -- and you are set for life. Why? Because the odds are on your side? That's how insurance always works.

Short of an overwhelming natural disaster, most of your customers eventually PAY IN much more than their losses will ever be. Indeed, even a natural disaster is not so big a threat as you might think -- because most insurance policies have built-in exceptions for what are legally called "acts of God."

Brando was even more fortunate. He didn't need to build his own agency. He had inherited it.

Hence, even as a young man, Brando didn't need to spend years making cold calls and knocking on doors to sell anything. He could just take care of existing clients, as well as the friends and family they often referred to him for new policies.

In effect, Brando had been handed almost a brass ring. And he was using it. He had plenty of time to explore other things in life beyond just making a living -- things like trying to start an annual theater festival right there in Flathead County.

Much like Luka, Brando had been obliged to take over the family business early. Brando's father hadn't become disabled, however. He had committed suicide.

Sadly, the person who commits suicide always hurts SO many others.

Maybe if the person contemplating taking his or her own life KNEW how many people they would hurt -- and how badly -- they would never do it.

Still sadder, perhaps, it is often done with the deliberate INTENTION of hurting someone.

In this case, Brando's father may have wanted to hurt just ONE person . . . the one who broke his heart.

Not surprisingly, like the son, the father, too, had had that animalistic grace and swagger, that catlike grace in his movements. He was also a smooth talker. Along with the fact that he was financially well off, those qualities sometimes attracted a FINE female companion.

When this particular fine damsel dumped him, Brando's old man had committed what the church says is always a MORTAL sin. Good for the church -- at least in this case.

Now Brando had to wonder if he was prone to do the same.

And, certainly, it had hit him hard when his father killed himself. It would do that to any man's son.

Maybe that was the reason Brando was now more interested in artistic dramas -- than in reality.

Sometimes reality leaves much to be desired.

Eve had persisted in her calling -- just in case there had been a cancellation, when another patient on the waiting list recovered, went elsewhere, or, yes, died waiting. That persistence had paid off. Luka now had an earlier appointment.

With Eve at his side, the brain surgeon at St. Peter's Health, the state's leading hospital in Helena, told Luka of a NEW and noninvasive treatment for cancer.

This new treatment was called "immunotherapy." That meant stimulating the patient's own immune system to attack and destroy the cancer cells.

As the surgeon explained, "It's a variation of DNA therapy.

The basic premise behind it is simple: Your DNA knows what BELONGS in your body -- and what does not."

This treatment was quite new, and -- accordingly -- there was very little basis to predict its chances of success in a particular instance.

In fact, as the brain surgeon emphasized, most of its applications so far had been used to treat cancer in less vital organs.

There appeared to have been only one instance of using it to treat a cancerous BRAIN tumor. And that patient had not recovered. He had died.

On the other hand, first of all, that patient's brain tumor was more advanced than Luka's. Second, Luka's local doctors had been correct. Given its location, his own brain tumor was inoperable.

Immunotherapy was not an operation. There would be no cutting to get to the tumor. It would be done through injections; just like getting a "shot" for any other illness.

What were the chances of success? And what would be the side effects of sending his DNA to fight something in his brain? No one knew.

Given that, as the surgeon advised, Luka may want to think about whether he really wanted to try this treatment.

Did he?

And what did Eve think?

15

LET YOUR LIGHT SO SHINE
BEFORE MEN . . . (MATTHEW 5:16)
(OR: WHAT GOES UP MAY WIN THE DAY)

I n deference to Teresa, whose compelling eyes had left no room for doubt, Rusty had withdrawn his entry into the "The Great Canyon Creek Leap."

That may have been a disappointment to his longstanding if often shell-shocked fans, but only a small one. With his smirk now broader than ever, and deservingly so, the county's favorite dare devil had come home **bearing gold** – the first-place medal in the "kicker" competition held the same day.

A "kicker," as you may recall, is a type of ramp that the snowboarder enters at high speed – to fly off into the air. And winning top prize in that competition was no small honor. Kickers, as noted earlier, were 1) the most difficult snow park structure to master, and 2) provided the greatest "air" to the accomplished rider.

Well, guess who got the biggest air that day?

Even Teresa, not always a fan of her husband's escapades, was both proud and impressed. "They SHOULD have given you a big fat **trophy** for that leap," she had argued. "Something more than that little medal."

"Nah, that would just set on a shelf somewhere," Rusty countered. "This medal I can wear EVERYWHERE." And for the next month, he would do exactly that.

It also seemed to go quite well with that patented smirk on his face, his now larger-than-ever calling card.

Teresa was visibly surprised when Jen asked, "Could you let Brando know I might be interested in him?"

As usual, Teresa's large and in charge blues eyes said it all. She was puzzled.

"Well maybe, Jen", said Rusty's wife -- and one of the community's go-to problem solvers.

Not having been back to the tundra that long, and having known Teresa only about a month, Jen had no way to anticipate what else her new friend would have to say.

"Is there a problem between you and Rod? Did you have a fight?"

"Well . . . not exactly," came the answer.

Seeing that Teresa was expecting a better answer, Jen was thinking about what to say next – if anything.

After all, at this point Jen didn't know Teresa that well -- and, more telling, perhaps, she wasn't so sure of what SHE herself knew about the problem.

As was her way, Jen had been relying on her intuition.

Yes, Jen's intuition about people was usually correct. That was her gift.

But USING that same normally reliable intuition, Jen also sensed that her new friend was both wise and determined to be helpful in such matters.

So she told Teresa the whole story about Rod and his trips to New England.

As has oft been said, two heads are better than one. And now there were two insightful females sharing and interpreting the facts of the case, the case of the trips to New England.

Snow, ice and even water itself are good insulators. For that reason, the fish in ponds and lakes rarely die in the winter. They just live down UNDER the ice.

The same is true in large rivers.

Even many mountain streams have fresh – and still running – water below the ice – if and when they finally freeze on the surface.

Of course, rapidly running "white water" mountain streams, famously challenging for canoe and kayak enthusiasts, are slow to freeze even on the surface. And they NEVER do freeze in some of their more torrential sections.

All of this Stacy knew very well. And she and Brando were doing just fine out in the remote vastness of the Flathead Indian Reservation. They had all the fish they needed to eat, usually harvested by chopping holes in a stream's ice – and just reaching down to grasp them with your hand. You needed no fishing lines or hooks. You just had to know where to find the fish. And how to grasp them so slowly they scarcely realized your hand was there.

Stacy also had her stashes of fruits, nuts and vegetables -- from wild strawberries to crab apples to native plums to chestnuts, from sweet root to wild asparagus to wild onions -- all harvested and stored during their seasons.

Certainly, there was no shortage of wood to burn. It was interesting to Brando, however, that Stacy never cut down a tree, not even a small one. Her people, she explained, used only the DEAD trees and branches that have fallen. It is the Pilgrim who cuts down healthy trees, like those trees have no right to live – like all of nature is just there for him to ravish.

That plentiful dead wood was also DRY, and perfect for burning, in any case. Sometimes outside, and sometimes inside her lodge, that wood not only served to cook the sweet root, other veggies and fish – but to keep both she and Brando warm. At nights and during storms, that dead firewood kept them warm as toast inside her A-frame skin-covered lodge.

Lush pelts, including two bearskins, also helped to keep them snug.

So did their joyously shared body heat, both when sleeping -- and in their embraces and purely natural acts of love.

"Forbidden fruit" was not a concept native Americans bought into.

And, despite all their modern wonders -- from TV to the internet, from fancy cars to flying machines – could any Pilgrim claim to have found ANYTHING better than sweet sexual love . . . in your chosen one's arms?

On the more mundane level, Brando's frostbite and other health issues stemming from his nearly lethal entrapment out in the frozen tundra, were history now. Yes, just as he had expected, Stacy was all the medicine that Brando might ever need, once he and she had bid their bold farewell to the county hospital.

Luka had insisted that Eve should continue her snowmobile racing. "I won't let you give up YOUR life trying to save mine," he told her. "Besides, watching you do your thing is good for my soul – and everyone else's."

In his own mind, Luka was thinking that he was but a tiny drop in an ongoing sea of human purposes -- all themselves only passing minutia in the larger order of nature's mysterious plan. Like anyone else, he had no right to deny Eve her own moment in nature's plan.

Did Luka have some kind of natural gift for understanding such matters? Or was it the **perspective** he had gained in the face of knowing he needed to do the right thing . . . right NOW, as there may be no tomorrow?

Yes, Eve had summed it up. Luka was now thinking much like a Buddhist monk.

But fortunately for them both, he had NOT taken that vow of celibacy. Unlike a real monk, he still gained inner strength from that "carnal knowledge" they shared in bed.

In the bible it said that David KNEW Bathsheba (which did not set well with her husband, Uriah the Hittite.)

But so and so KNEW so and so was only the bible's way of

saying that someone got laid. And usually that turned out quite WELL, thank you. After all, if Eve hadn't "known" Adam none of us would be here, would we?

Even "bible thumpers" had to concede that, did they not?

So shoot the messenger, if you will: If anything, in the face of his brain tumor -- and the dizzy spells reminding him of it daily -- Luka was now even more often UP (so to speak) for sharing that forbidden fruit with Eve.

Whether because of Luka's insistence – or just her own NEED to let off a little steam -- Eve had entered the biggest snowmobile race Flathead county had ever hosted.

And that was saying a lot.

Brando's vision of starting a soon to be acclaimed Theater Festival in Flathead County might be a delusion, but Western Montana was pretty much the snowmobile racing capital of the nation – if not the WORLD.

Those proud to enter races wherever was second would likely KNOW that.

They were calling it "The Big Sky Challenge." And there were many sponsors promoting this race, including major players in Montana's large and thriving TOURIST industry.

Some of the biggest NAMES in snowmobile RACING would also be there, from manufacturers like Polaris, Ski-Doo and Artic Cat. . . to RACERS themselves, including Justin Broberg (Polaris), Logan Christian (Artic Cat), and Robbie Malinoski (Ski-Doo).

Daring as they come, accustomed to winning, and a brazen Tomboy from day one – and now with Luka so intent upon her DOING her thing -- Eve did not intend to disappoint.

As always, too, she would have a natural edge, weighing in

at MANY pounds less than nearly all her competitors, however famous.

TMK and Michele had returned from their winter excursion up to the high country. Upon reaching the border of the Flathead Indian Reservation, they had stopped at the trading post just inside the gate, picking up blankets, pottery items, and leather goods – all handmade by members of the several Indian tribes to whom that land had been bestowed in exchange for peace in the Treaty of Hellgate on July 16, 1855.

TMK's father had told him several times that the best billfold he had ever owned was one made by the hands of those Native Americans. It was almost indestructible; lasting for over 15 years. Like his father before him, TMK had bought one of those real leather wallets on this trip, along with some dancing boots – one pair for him, and one MUCH smaller pair for Michelle. Hers were decorated with beautiful feathers at their sides, which the sales maiden declared to be Cape May Warbler's and Kingfisher's, as well as with beaver fur at their tops.

They could use those blankets and the pottery items when they got home. But unbeknownst to either Michelle or the sales maiden, TMK had plans for those dancing boots . . . that same day.

Like most everything in Western Montana, the Flathead Reservation DIDN'T officially close for the winter. It was open, if you could get there. And that didn't just mean the trading post.

With 1938 square miles of area, and being quite sparsely populated, it was prime country for Daisy to play in the snow. And play she did. Who needs roads when you have Daisy?

They also stopped to set up a quick campfire; not with the intent to stay for the night, but just as a place to breath in the fresh air – and meld with nature.

Well that, and a place to USE those dancing boots. TMK had visited the reservation years before with his father and his uncle, and they had been lucky enough to visit during one of the Native Americans' POW WOWs. Unlike what one might guess, a Pow Wow today was not a meeting or any kind of political affair. It was just a celebration – a DANCING celebration. And just like everywhere across the American Midwest and West today, regardless of the tribe or tribes sponsoring one, today's Pow Wows were attended by Native Americans of any and ALL nations or tribes. They were also open to visiting Pilgrims, who were welcomed – and encouraged to JOIN in the dancing.

The Indians believed that such dancing was good for the soul, the mind, and the body. They were almost certainly correct.

TMK may not have remembered the dancing steps exactly right, but he remembered them – and some of the chants that accompanied them – well enough for their purposes. Following his lead, Michelle and TMK danced around that campfire as much like Native Americans as they could muster. And it DID serve their minds and body's well. Their souls, too, they were sure.

Rod was due to return from New England tomorrow. Further, in his phone call telling Jen of this, he had also said that his business there was concluded. So he would be back to STAY now.

The ultimate picture was yet to be determined, but it appeared distinctly possible that Teresa had saved Jen AND Rod from a nasty and tragically ill-fated ending based on a case of mistaken intuition.

Before asking Teresa if she could put in a word to Brando of her interest and availability, Jen had been planning to just leave Rod standing at the gate in the airport, wondering where she might be.

Yes, in addition to her intuitive gifts, Jen had a TEMPER. But what woman doesn't? Especially when she feels betrayed?

As is often attributed to Shakespeare, "Hell hath no fury like a woman scored." (In fact, historians trace this saying to a slightly longer line written by William Congreve, a playwright and early *student* of William Shakespeare: "Heav'n has no rage, like love to hatred turn'd, nor Hell a fury like a woman scorn'd (*The Morning Bride*, 1697)."

But, after talking it over with Teresa, Jen realized that Rod had actually been very good to her up to now. They also made a good TEAM. While saving Brando from freezing to death out in the middle of nowhere had been inspired – and just in time – by HER strong intuition, she could not have saved him without the help of Rod and his hot air balloon. And give the man credit: at that time he barely knew Jen, and had been making a leap of faith to believe in her – and go to all that trouble.

Perhaps even more worthy of remembering, there likely wouldn't BE a Brando now -- if not for Rod's willingness to humor Jen on the basis of her hunch about Brando freezing out there. It would seem doubly unfair – and likely bad Karma -- to dump Rod so she could take up with a man who *wouldn't even be alive without his noble intervention.*

So Jen would be there waiting at the airport gate for Rod. Was she still suspicious that he may have been cheating on her? Yes, she was. Her intuition was still a gift she had learned to value. But now she would give him a chance to prove himself.

Or to HANG himself, as the case might be.

16

. . .He that hath Mercy upon the Poor, happy is he (Proverbs 14:21)
(or: They Who Give Not Are Poor in Spirit)

It was truly good to live in Montana. If you told those in more urban states ALL the reasons for that, they would probably think you were a bit touched in the head, or certainly a touch biased.

Such a bias might obtain, but ONE of the reasons for feeling good about Montana was this: Its people were not just into "taking it big" like TMK, big skies and equally big landscapes; they also had big HEARTS.

Even *politicians* there -- not an occupation normally regarded as honestly caring – were kindly by nature. A current example had just hit the local news media.

It was an announcement that would WARM the big hearts of Montanans.

Valentine's Day was close on the horizon. While the poet Chaucer in the Middle Ages first associated the holiday with romantic love, that day of the year had been one to celebrate human procreation even centuries before that.

That was about *fertility rituals,* WAY back when the idea of human OVER-population would have been unthinkable.

Eventually, Christianity arose, and the Pope banned fertility rituals as "pagan." He decreed the day, instead, one to celebrate St. Valentine, the patron saint of lovers, epileptics and bookkeepers.

If that seems like a strange combination of things for one saint to represent, well . . . Popes can decree things as they please.

TODAY, as any school child knows, Valentine's Day is represented by HEARTS. Every elementary school classroom is decorated with LOTS of hearts on that day – and children delight in giving heart-shaped valentine cards and candies to ALL their classmates. So, most fundamentally, that day now means SHARING and CARING.

Of course, on the same day, those heart-shaped decorations also adorn the walls and windows of everything from homes for the elderly . . . to post offices, grocery stores, restaurants and bars. In short, fortunately enough, we need NEVER outgrow that sharing and caring feeling of Valentine's Day, a feeling we discovered in elementary school.

And politicians? Well, at least in Montana, they never outgrew that feeling either. In fact, this year the Governor's Office was sponsoring a "Love is the Answer" drive – collecting donations to fight poverty throughout the state. Further, they were asking folks to nominate people in their own circles of friends to be group leaders. The promotional theme was "Team Up for Love."

The Governor's charity drive even had a theme song:

> She calls out to the man in the street
> "Sir, can you help me?
> It's gettin' cold and there's nowhere to sleep
> Is there somewhere you can tell me?"
> Oh, think twice
> 'Cause there's another day for you and me in paradise
> Oh, think twice
> 'Cause there's another day for you
> You and me in paradise

(Lyrics from "Another Day In Paradise." By Phil Collins. Released in 1989.)

Those in Luka and Eve's local circle -- those who attended the parties Teresa often threw at her and Rusty's place – ALL knew one thing: They were among the financially fortunate.

While people elsewhere may be cynical and prone to blame the poor for BEING poor, most Montanans were not.

Luka and Eve were ready to respond, to become ACTIVE participants in this statewide drive.

So were most of their friends.

The "Love Is the Answer" statewide Valentine's drive to help the poor was an uplifting event for all. In her training to become a nurse, Eve had learned from a certain psychology professor that helping others makes us feel better ourselves. There was even evidence that this feeling, this psychological BENEFIT, also translated into physical health gains, including an enhanced working of our immune systems.

FEELING better, it seemed, was not just a feeling in one's mind. The mind and the BODY, as philosophers had long insisted, are NOT separate realms. Just as pain in one's body is experienced as a negative in one's mind, a body feeling good makes the mind feel good, as well.

And vice versa, a mind feeling good is a tonic for the rest of one's body.

But none of that had surprised Eve. Why did she choose to go into NURSING in the first place? Because, somehow, she had already known that helping OTHERS was what would make her happy. The evidence, as she had learned from that professor, said it could make her HEALTHIER, too.

In her and Luka's case, this particular HELPING OTHERS project was even MORE timely. They both needed time to think about what the brain surgeon had said. Did they want to TRY that immunotherapy to fight Luka's brain tumor? Even when the ONLY other case of doing that had ended badly?

That was LOT to chew on. They knew they should think that over for a while.

What better to do with that time -- then to look beyond themselves, joining in the governor's drive to help the poor?

As an expert on cosmetics, products at which she excelled in marketing, Jen was inspecting, trimming, and touching up her fingernails with the BEST combination strengthener and polish on the market. In fact, she did that EVERY day, just as she practiced a daily facial care regimen, with the best and mildest cleansers, toners and moisturizers.

Those rituals were NOT just for her appearance, which was always glowing. Like Luka, Jen had learned that following daily ROUTINES was good for your attitude on life.

When things were disturbing in your world – like Rod's suspicious trips to New England – these routines became even more helpful.

People may not realize it, but Jen's consistently COMPOSED and always outwardly AT EASE manner was one of the things that made her so attractive. That attractiveness ran deeper than her appeal to the prurient interests of men on the prowl.

It wasn't that Jen had anything against men on the prowl, necessarily, she just wanted to be MORE than that to the world. She wanted to be a LADY, a term that once had meant so much – and still did to a discerning few. Indeed, even to those who didn't know what being a lady was all about, that gracious feminine composure and unflappable poise was both delightful and compelling.

And at BEING that lady, Jen was uncommonly – and consistently -- successful.

What an intelligent MAN needed to realize was that in her presence it was only proper to act like a GENTLEMAN.

Those were the only men who had a chance with Lady Jen-Jen.

Jen's composure was something she could always bank on. When she met Rod at the airport, Jen was not going to pretend to ardent feelings of warmth she didn't have for him now. He was a question mark to her at this point, and just being that composed and attractively serene lady was quite enough to offer him now. Quite enough, indeed, she thought.

There was MORE that Jen had decided. She wouldn't even extend her arms . . . to offer Rod a hug at the airport. Hey, he'd be lucky that she was even showing up! That was her attitude now.

Nor would she pick up one of his bags this time. That was HIS damned job. A lady was to be pampered – not expected to act like a pack mule.

That was her plan, and she was resolved to STICK with it.

Yes, despite Teresa's magnanimous intervention, for which Rod should be thankful – IF he deserved it – Jen was still angry.

> I just wanna throw my phone away
> Find out who is really there for me
> You ripped me off your love was cheap
> Was always tearing at the seams
>
> I fell deep, you let me down
> But that was then and this is now, now look at me
> This is the part of me
> That you're never gonna ever take away from me, no!

(Lines from "Part of Me." By Katy Perry. Released 2012.)

It would be up to Rod to figure that out.
Maybe he would. Maybe he wouldn't.

This time the gathering at Rusty and Teresa's place was BOTH a holiday celebration AND a mobilization effort for the "Love is the Answer" charity drive announced and promoted by the Governor's Office. Valentine's Day was still a week off, but it wasn't unusual to celebrate a holiday early, not in Montana. Like The Mighty Quinn and his month-long birthday parties, the RUGGED people who thrived in that challenging weather and a difficult-to-navigate landscape were nearly ALWAYS up for a party.

It seems that the fewer people per square mile, the more we appreciate and like to gather with the neighbors we have.

But along with all the Valentine's decorations and the obligatory special attention to NEW couples, including Rod and Jen, now back together at least for the moment (new love being considered the most deliciously romantic), this was also a meeting to ***get organized.***

After first teasing TMK about Michelle again, "that Beauty with the Beast," as they all liked to put it now, he was nominated and elected to be their "Team Leader," in the statewide charity drive.

Given TMK's occupation, foreman for the county's powerline crew, that was not surprising. While Rod knew that powerlines were the number one threat to hot-air balloons, TMK knew something else: When someone, some family, or some new business decided to move out into the tundra, outside the limits of what passed for a town there, getting powerlines out to them was no small challenge. Such were the realities of that beautiful Montana landscape.

That was the OTHER side of having 314 named mountains in Flathead County.

Once in place, maintaining those powerlines, which often went down in storms, was not for the timid either. Climbing a powerline pole ANYWHERE was an athletic endeavor. Hanging off the side of a mountain to replace one of those poles, was only for those with BIG gonads . . . be those organs residing in an exceptionally daring male OR female.

It just came with the territory, of course, that TMK would not ask anyone he supervised to do what HE hadn't done himself.

On the biggest challenges out there, he would call his own number, doing that especially dangerous job himself.

Mighty as he was, however, TMK was not good at giving speeches.

Fear not. Should anyone in the circle doubt the NEED for this drive, Eve had this to say:

> "Doctors and nurses see it all the time. So many patients don't come in for help until it's too late. Why? Because they're afraid of the bills. They think they can't afford it. And they may be right. We now have Medicaid in this state, a federal program that was supposed to pay part of the medical bills for the poor. But it doesn't work so well. Many don't qualify for Medicaid, and many others can't afford the part that Medicaid doesn't pay. They all know people who have lost their life savings to medical bills.
>
> And those are the lucky ones. Many are literally starving. So are their children."

While Rod and Jen where there TOGETHER at this combined Valentine's party and charity-drive organizer, those two were not at all cuddly. They weren't sitting close to one another, nor even talking much.

It was perhaps well to remember that both Rod and Jen were NEW to the tundra and this circle of friends. Who else would either of them come with?

Rod, as he may or not realize, was on probation, so far as Jen was concerned. Then his phone rang.

Then it rang again. He didn't seem eager to answer it. And just let it keep ringing.

"Who's calling, Rod?" asked Jen-Jen. "Maybe you should check to see."

"I know who it is," the wayward one now back from New England said. "It's some damned *thieves* who are trying to sell me an outrageously expensive insurance policy . . . that they say covers me and any passengers when I'm up in my balloon. They call all the time."

Without a word, Jen's face and now coldly distant eyes said it loud and clear: She was not buying that line.

Rod barely noticed that nonverbal thumbs down, however. He had already detected that Jen was not one bit happy with him. Now he almost wished he could kick himself – and not for that reason alone.

"I never should have gone to Boston," he said, almost to himself, it seemed. But then looking at Jen, as apparently forlorn as a man could be, he added, "Those Ivy Leaguers back there have the money, and I wanted their business, but it comes at TOO high a price."

"I wanted . . . I wanted . . . to try to make it big," he continued, haltingly. "Now everyone seems to think I'm a fool. Even you, I guess."

17

HOW MUCH BETTER IS IT TO GET WISDOM THAN GOLD . . . (PROVERBS 16:16)
(OR: WHICH WAY NOW?)

Rusty and God were having a talk. "I've been wondering, God," Rusty asked, "Why are some people poor and other people rich?"

God responded, "That's like asking why Tigers have stripes and Leopards have spots. That's just the way they are. You could also ask why a Mayfly lives only one day when whales often live over 200 years. Or you might ask why some people can run fast and others can't. Or why some people can jump high and others have . . . well, white man's disease."

Now Rusty was grinning to himself. It seemed that God had a sense of humor.

God concluded with, "Wouldn't it be boring if all the critters – and all the people -- were the same?"

"Oh, I wasn't complaining, God. I like the world just they way it is. And I usually have lots of fun."

"Yes, I've noticed that, son," God now observed.

Rusty couldn't see God's face, but only heard his words, and he had to wonder how the creator had MEANT that last comment. "I hope that's okay, God," he offered plaintively. "Sure it is, Rusty," came the answer. "In fact, I find you entertaining."

Of course, Rusty's little chat with God was just in a dream. When the county's favorite dare devil awakened, he didn't know what to make of it. But so it goes with dreams. Most of them don't make sense. And neither did this one.

Or did it?

It just came with TMK's job -- supervising the crews that installed and maintained all the powerlines in the county. He knew all the streets, highways, secondary and altogether BACK roads out there – as well as all the businesses, homes and ranches lying along each street, highway and byway

This was highly useful information, aiding TMK in assigning routes to his team members in their all-volunteer unit of benevolent "soldiers," part of the statewide "Love Is the Answer" charity drive.

TMK's troops were soon out there knocking on doors, intending to miss not a one. Since it was still February, they would have to be mindful of weather conditions, to be sure. But they were all hearty souls, and knew how to drive in less than ideal conditions.

In just a week, that team had collected nearly $120,000 in donations, some of that tracing to the persistence, persuasiveness, local popularity, and charm of the team members. But more of it standing as abundant evidence of the aforementioned **generosity** of Western Montanans, as a whole.

Jen admitted to Rod, "I had a feeling that you were having an affair . . . that you were seeing another woman out there in Boston. And my intuition is usually right."

Rod had to smile, knowing that Jen was not so far wrong. But he also knew that whole subject was a potential minefield. Finally, now smiling again, he allowed, "Well, I wasn't fooling around with anyone. I promise you that. But there WAS someone there who intrigued me. But only because she reminded me so much of YOU. She even seemed to have that sixth sense of yours . . . We only talked a couple of times. But she said. 'I can tell you have another woman on your mind when you look at me.'"

Jen was listening carefully.

And Rod fully realized anything else he'd say on that subject had better be short and sweet. He added only, "She was right, of course."

Jen could tell that her not so wayward man was telling the truth. But she had a question: "So which one of us do you prefer, Mr. Man- of-the-World?"

The sarcasm in how Jen had phrased that question was NOT

lost on the man now trying to defend himself, but he wanted to tell her his real feelings. He wanted her to know.

Isn't that the way it always is – when a man is in love?

"I want the REAL you, Jen," was his answer to her.

He added, "I want you . . .I need you . . . and I love you. Yes, I LOVE you, Jen-Jen."

Luka knew he couldn't be counted on to drive alone now, especially not late in the day. It was in the evenings that his dizzy spells were the most frequent and disorienting. And he had to admit, at least to himself, that those spells were becoming worse.

Still not wishing to be viewed as an invalid in need of sympathy, Luka didn't go into detail. He just let TMK know that he would much prefer to take his turns at door-knocking for the charity drive on the weekends, *during the daylight hours.*

That was another time when they could expect to find most folks at home. Luka just said, "Lately, I've been having trouble driving in the evenings, after the sun goes down." And gave no further explanation.

Of course, there was a larger issue at stake. Quite apart from any driving, those worsening dizzy spells – including hallucinations – were telling Luka that his brain tumor appeared to be becoming a more urgent problem.

He still hadn't wanted to tell Eve about the hallucinations; not wanting to worry her with all that, but the inevitable happened. Eve dropped in to visit Luka one evening after her shift at the hospital was over, *and he thought she was someone else.* He wasn't sure who, but she seemed like a zombie from some kind of Halloween horror movie, or maybe a monster from outer space. Damn, he'd better quit watching those crazy sci-fi films, he told himself!

So now Luka had to admit -- both to himself AND to Eve -- that his symptoms were getting worse.

The doctors had said that would happen sooner or later. They just didn't know when.

When Rod had poured out his real feelings to Jen – when he had confessed that he LOVED her – the sarcasm had left her face almost immediately.

After a short frown, Jen had looked at him with only SWEET devotion in her eyes, much as she might look at a child in her care. Especially since he had already declared that going to Boston was a big mistake -- and that he now looked like a fool -- she could see that Rod wasn't just telling the truth . . . he was also VULNERABLE at this moment.

He needed her . . . to be there for him.

It was now or never, she thought. Besides, the man now professing his love . . . had hit squarely upon her weak spot. Or was it another one of her strengths?

Jen was an empath. She could really FEEL others' pain. That probably came right along with being so intuitive about other peoples' intentions.

"Oh, Rod," she breathed, "I love you, too."

Then he reached for her -- and relished the way she accepted his kiss ... surrendering to it deeply and completely, sealing their renewed bond.

It was fair to say that the bond between Rod and Jen-Jen was now stronger than ever.

As the poets seemed to know, 'tis love nearly lost that is savored most dearly.

At Luka's insistence, Eve had NOT ONLY entered "The Big Sky Challenge," the most widely promoted snowmobile race ever hosted in Flathead County, but she had also managed to find time to practice.

Because she had been devoting most of her time -- when not at work as a hospital nurse -- to watching over Luka, Eve had not entered any races for a while. This was despite the fact that it had been the HEIGHT of the racing season.

Nor, of course, had Eve been to the track lately, to dash off any time-trial laps.

But she was practicing now.

And Luka was always there WITH her. She was his pride and joy, not to mention his inspiration at this point. As the lucky recipient of Eve's determined will to win – at about anything she set her mind to – Luka was her number one ADMIRER, and for reasons well beyond his partner's beauty or their shared sexual chemistry.

To Luka, Eve was the shit!

And, yes, he had insisted that she should enter this race, and not give up HER life trying to save his.

She may have needed to practice, to remind and recondition her muscles to their highest state of symmetry with her snowmobile at racing speed, but Eve was still holding some KEY "cards in this game," as the old expression would have it.

In addition to her light weight, Eve had another BIG advantage. This was "home court" for her. She knew this track like the back of her hand.

Although she was probably not thinking about it, Eve also held TWO other cards in this game coming up – the biggest race in the history of the county.

First of all, "home court" meant more than being intimately familiar with the county racetrack's racing SURFACE, in all of its peculiar patches of soft and harder, high and lower spots, and the exact bend of its turns. Eve, *as a smart better would know,* could also expect to have by far the largest CHEERING section on that big race day.

Second, it is only fair to say that on the appointed race day, all the fans – and the racers, too -- would come to FEEL it: The ANNOUCER, the booming voice calling every detail of the race, was one of Eve's biggest fans.

It's ALSO only fair to say that the announcer -- a local gentleman, of course -- probably admired the track's fan favorite for more than her racing skills.

Eve was a hottie, after all.

And what's wrong with that?

> You'd think that people would have had enough of silly love songs
> I look around me and I see it isn't so
> Some people want to fill the world with silly love songs
> And what's wrong with that
>
> I'd like to know
>
> (Lines from "Silly Love Songs." By Paul McCartney & Wings. Released 1984.)

Eve had agreed to be in that big race. Just as she had agreed not to tell their friends of Luka's tumor; just as she had scoured the region's hospital websites searching for the best brain surgeons; just as she had pestered their staffs relentlessly until she had scored that earliest possible appointment with the surgeon, the one who had apprised him of that cutting-edge immunotherapy option, after confirming that, yes, his tumor was otherwise inoperable. And, yes, just as she had checked on him every single day since – all out of an AMAZING love.

No wonder she was his hero.

And she didn't plan to disappointment him.

Of course, as the poet Robert Burns first warned, *"The best laid plans of mice and men often go awry."* (Yes, that is the gist of his thought, as it has long been loosely translated from Scottish idiom of the day in his poem "To a Mouse," in which Burns actually wrote, "The best laid schemes o' Mice an' Men, Gang aft agley. An' lea'e us nought but grief an' pain, For promis'd joy!" November, 1785.)

In Eve and Luka's case, there was also a proviso -- if unstated, yet clear to each of their irreparably entangled hearts. A decision must soon be made about that immunotherapy. Would it prove to be the right decision? Or would it only bring their rapt devotion to an even quicker end?

Just this much appeared to be certain. Luka had gained more than *inspiration* from Eve -- and more than a joy of the heart that could not but be a healing elixir of its own, to some degree.

She had become a PART of him . . . and that part of him was now determined to face every life challenge head on.

18

THERE IS NO FEAR IN LOVE . . . (JOHN 4:18)
(OR: MOMENTS OF TRUTH AT HAND)

Nothing came easy in Western Montana. A winter storm had blown in, bringing 4 feet of snow in less than 24 hours.

It wasn't a record. But it was enough to put virtually all travel on hold. Even Daisy couldn't be expected to get through that much snow.

One thing was obvious: the state's largest-ever snowmobile race, "The Big Sky Challenge," had to be postponed. The many sponsors and promotors were promising to get the race rescheduled -- for early or mid-March. That wouldn't be easy, however. Not when SO many big-name participants, their teams and their fans were committed to upcoming snowmobile races elsewhere. It was the height of the season, after all.

As for Eve, right now she couldn't even get to the county track to practice.

On the other hand, that did NOT preclude practicing out in the open tundra. Indeed, after that blizzard, a snowmobile was about the ONLY way to get anywhere in Flathead County.

Besides, new snow only made it more beautiful out there in the tundra, with everything now looking as stunning and exquisite as a vintage ermine fur . . . and all the mountain peaks appearing to stand guard over that unmolested Montana domain, now regally blanketed in a thick, ermine-like robe as far as the eye could see.

With the sun gleaming on all that fresh whiteness, the tundra now looked even more vast and majestic.

To locals, that was an invitation writ large.

An outsider might think it was a time for Montanans to hunker down inside. But that was not in their nature.

"You should still practice," said Luka to his amazing counterpart, an Eve much more wondrous than any scripture had anticipated. "The race will be ON again soon. And you will STUN them, My Love."

As Eve had realized quickly, Luka was NOT the average man.

He didn't mind taking a back seat to her at times . . . when she so richly deserved a starring role. Some self-important disc jockey in Denver had recently broken up with Taylor Swift – because she was getting more press than he was.

How stupid was that?

A REAL man would not be troubled by a woman who attracted attention, especially when it was HIS arm she preferred.

Luka and Eve now raced across that tundra together, he behind her on the same ultrafast machine.

The manufacturers warned that passengers should only be carried on snowmobiles designed for two, those with an extra seat or a longer seat, as well as rear handgrips for the passenger; warning that otherwise, riding "two up" will change the vehicle's center of gravity and affect the operator's ability to steer.

But Eve was both ultralight AND an expert at racing these machines.

With just the addition of a strapped-on pad behind her, and some hand grips Luka had mounted himself, as the handy fellow he was, he and Eve were in NO danger out there . . . speeding across that regally adorned expanse, cloaked in its new mantle of white.

The only REAL danger confronting the starstruck pair blazing across Montana's winter tundra was the one inside Luka's head, that ever more menacing tumor.

Were they being blind to the facts?

Not quite. Right now, they couldn't even GET TO the hospital over in Helena, where the brain surgeon could start the first immunotherapy treatments, should they decide to proceed with that.

The roads wouldn't be open for days.

But they COULD call the doctor, should they decide to schedule an appointment for that first treatment. After all, the good doctor had given them his personal phone number, encouraging them to call him at any time.

In a word, that surgeon was exceptional, and in more ways than one.

But it was up to his new patient and his amazing mate. Would they call?

Should they call?

The big storm wasn't just a local thing. It had left about as much snow – perhaps even a foot or so MORE – up in the higher elevation of the Flathead Indian Reservation.

Stacy and Brando had no snowmobile up there. But they DID have snowshoes, handmade and native to Stacy's people. Indeed, Native Americans had snowshoes long before any Pilgrim had set foot on this continent.

Brando, entirely back to health, was also invigorated by living, *"out in nature, under the sky, the way God intended"* as he put it.

As for intentions, Brando still wanted to finish work on his huge outdoor amphitheater, but he had NO plans to give up his life with Stacy. He was trying to convince her to JOIN him in that ambitious project.

"T'was written in the Great Spirit's plan," he exhorted his Indian princess, "that we will bring people back to the OUTDOORS, back to open-air theater as the Ancient Greek's began it -- and the way it was MEANT to be."

Brando delivered his words along with magnificent hand, arm and facial gestures, attesting to the wonderment that, as his large and abundantly expressive eyes alone fully conveyed, he believed in with every ounce of his being.

Sometimes Stacy just had to laugh. Her chosen man WAS a bit noisy and flamboyant at times (a good part of the time, truth be said); much like a noisy Blue Jay; making such a fuss as to DISTURB the other birds and wild critters in the forest.

Like most Native Americans, Stacy tended to think it was best to *blend in* with nature, and not disturb its balance – rather than trying to "CONQUER" nature as many a destructive Pilgrim had phrased it. But she could also see that Brando was NOT one of those Pilgrims, not blind to the ways of nature; but much TAKEN with it; and not a destructive fellow, in any way.

He just wasn't meant to take a low profile. Brando was meant to expound and to EXPRESS. He was an ARTIST of sorts – and his natural artistic gift happened to be in "the performing arts" as they were called.

Yes, he could certainly put on a performance.

Brando's penchant for portraying larger-than-life dramatic scenes wasn't so foreign to Stacy's world. Native American peoples had long enjoyed storytelling, especially in the venue of what in English were called "ghost stories." Unlike what that phrase might conjure up to the Pilgrim mind, those stories were not typically of scary "monsters," but of more friendly creatures from the spirit world.

Often those spirts took the form of animals, except they talked and otherwise took on human-like behaviors.

Many times the "ghosts" in these Native American tales were helpful to the humans they befriended, even saving them from dangers. Other times these spirit figures were simply amusing, betraying some of the same silly faults as humans themselves.

Stacy knew something that made her smile. One of the "ghost stories" told among the Flathead Indians featured a Blue Jay.

Blue Jays Skinny Legs – A Flathead Legend

It happened a long time ago, before the arrival of the White brothers / sisters. There was a chief who had a very beautiful daughter. He wanted to make sure that she married a strong and healthy man. As the young men began to come around to flirt with his daughter, he became worried. He decided to reduce the odds by having a race. He informed all the young men that the one with the strongest legs could marry his daughter.

Coyote was crafty and a good runner with a lot of power, so he came first. He showed how long his legs were and how fast he could run. Then Deer came, a very handsome and strong buck. He showed how powerful his legs were at jumping, although they were somewhat knotted up. Then Grizzly Bear came along. Bear stood up and growled so everyone could see that he had very powerful and strong legs. So he claimed the girl.

But Blue Jay hollered that it was not fair, that others should still be considered. While the others were showing their legs, he hid behind an old log, where he had gathered a lot of tree moss and used clay to pack it around his legs. They looked larger and stronger than anyone's, even bigger than Grizzly Bears. But to sweeten the pot, Blue Jay also offered all kinds of beautiful feathers he had obtained from all of his different bird relations.

The old chief was fooled by this and let his daughter go with him. Blue Jay had to carry his new wife across the stream in order to reach his tepee on the other side. As he began the hard journey, the water softened the moss and clay, so they fell from his legs.

When he climbed up on the other side of the stream bank, everyone began to laugh. Grizzly Bear came down and claimed his prize, and with his strong legs carried his new wife up the side of the mountain.

Anytime he tries to come back and visit, the Blue Jay will start squawking all over the forest, and he makes a terrible noise. He does this because he is jealous and doesn't like to be laughed at.

(Source: https://www.firstpeople.us/FP-Html-Legends/ BluejaysSkinnyLegs-Flathead.html)

Stacy was quite familiar with this old Flathead story.

In another way, too, Brando's dramatic way of telling his stories was not so foreign to Stacy's world. All of these Native American ghost stories were part of an oral tradition. They had not been written down. And much of the entertainment value of the story came from the talent of the storyteller. In most cases, this was an elder, but not just ANY elder. Like the medicine man or woman, the storyteller was normally born into that role, passed on by his or her parent or grandparent, *after mastering the craft.*

That craft included skills to keep the listener's attention.

In brief, the storyteller wasn't just a repository of remembered words, but of showmanship.

Strangely enough, all of this was VERY much like the craft of an actor, a thespian; just as in the days of the Ancient Greeks. First, the actor (or storyteller) had not written or otherwise invented the script. He or she had MEMORIZED words carefully chosen by someone else. And, in both the case of the actor and the Native American storyteller, it wasn't some rough or approximate rendering of the story they provided – but the EXACT SAME WORDS each time the story or script was performed.

Then there was the SECOND similarity, the one brought up by Brando's dramatic ways. Both the thespian and the storyteller were expected to render the story with powerful nuance in voice and gestures – thus making it seem larger than life.

Mindful of the fact that women no longer wished to be called actresses, or even heroines – but simply actors and heroes – Brando was keen to Stacy's feedback.

He feared no scorn. Nor did he doubt himself.

It was simple. He saw Stacy as fully his equal, and wanted her opinion.

Stacy didn't count Brando's dream out.

She sensed that he MAY be onto something larger than himself, much larger . . . something that he could bring to others . . . the joy of LIVING that exquisite drama, something more compelling than the average dreary life, if only on stage.

Those Ancient Greek playwrights, INVENTORS of drama much larger than dreary lives, have lived on for so many centuries FOR A REASON.

Just as had the ghost stories told by Native Americans.

Brando knew that much. So did Stacy.

It was late, time for Luka to be asleep. But his mind was not his own now, not this late in the evening. Words of a song were in his head.

Feels like the end
When you're closer to losing your dreams
Than losing a friend
Flying blind
I'm shooting into the dark
Who will I find? . . .

I swear I'll tear down every wall
Love conquers all

(Lyrics from "Love Conquers All." By Deep Purple. Released 2006.)

"Love conquers all." That was a timeless theme, echoed in so many songs.

Could all those songs be wrong?

"Love conquers all?" Where did that crazy idea come from anyway? It sounded like some kind of religious notion to Luka. But that was not the case. It didn't come from scripture or any other religious source, but from an Ancient Roman poet, Virgil. That still famous poet was not into religion but human LOVE.

Specifically, the phrase derives from Virgil's Eclogues X.69: "Omnia vincit amor et nos cedamus amori," which is usually translated to mean "love conquers all, let us all yield to love."

And MAYBE the poet was right. After more than 2,000 years, he still lives in our hearts – and precisely because of the power of his poems extolling love.

Luka could finally sleep now.

He thought Virgil's point was beyond a pragmatic, problem-solving mentality; beyond the realm of the mechanical devises he sold and maintained. And also beyond what any doctor may or may not be able to cure. We all die physically. But some still live in other hearts . . . beyond any physical limits.

Luka believed he was one such blessed soul. He may die physically yet live on.

Because of Eve, there was little doubt.

There may have been another line or two that Virgil had not written. It may be that SOME love conquers still more than he thought.

In his slumber, Luka was hearing applause.

19

BEYOND SCRIPTURE OR SCRIPT:
IT IS WRITTEN, BUT SOME HEARTS
SAYETH MORE THAN WORDS

Rod's plan had seemed like a winner. It had boasted Montana-sized promise. But his vision of making a small fortune providing wealthy Ivy Leaguers with balloon rides out in Big Sky country had fallen flat.

Those Eastern sons and daughter of privilege couldn't HELP but be captivated by Montana's wonders . . . as viewed in their vastness from that overhead 360-degree view.

It was a win-win, Rod had thought.

Sadly, it had become instead a lose-lose.

Those New Englanders, so sure they already knew EVERYTHING, had never given Rod's plan a chance.

He was holding a few cards, however; all in the person of Jen.

With her marketing savvy, as triply supplemented by 1) college courses on the subject, 2) her appealing ladylike, always composed presence, along with 3) her uncanny intuitive "sixth sense" about people – Jen might be the ONE person who could indeed, "sell ice to the Eskimos."

To H with those Boston rich boys; there were plenty of other tourists – as well both locals and those in Montana's own towns and cities -- to whom to market those hot-air balloon rides.

Or as Jen-Jen put, "Don't you worry, Rod. I KNOW how wonderful it is up there in your balloon. And I can sell anything I believe in."

The snowmobile race, The Big Sky Challenge, had been rescheduled, although on a tentative basis. While the sponsors and promoters had hoped to schedule that make-up event by mid-March, other commitments by racers and sponsors had precluded re-setting the date for the race during the height of the season.

The big race was now set for April 6. That was a Saturday, which was the best day of the week for a large turnout. It was tentative, however, as they could not be sure of sufficient snow that late in the season.

On the other hand, so far … it had been an especially snowy year, and if the snow remained in their favor, it would be the LAST big race of the campaign. And whoever won would stand to prevail -- throughout the off season -- as the reigning champ of what they were still billing as "The Biggest Ever" event of its kind.

With Jen firmly on his side, Rod was heartened. More than that, he BELIEVED in Jen; just as much as she believed in him. He believed that she could indeed successfully market rides in his beloved balloon. And why not? She was so persuasive – and she was right. Balloon rides out over the Montana tundra were breathtakingly beautiful.

Anything that breathtaking was not only an attractive prospect – but prone to bring people back over and over. In that respect, it was like skydiving. Many who do it become devotees. They want more and MORE of it.

It was only to be expected that SOME of those devotees would dream of owning and flying their own teardrops over the tundra. But VERY few would be able to afford that. Nearly all the enthusiasts would be obliged to settle for rides.

Luka was glad to hear that the big snowmobile race had been rescheduled. "That's a winner, Eve. It's good that you've been practicing. I just know that the smart money has to be on you . . . to win it ALL."

"Well, Luka. I guess we will see -- if the snow holds up."

In truth, Eve was more focused on another matter. After she

had learned of Luka's hallucinations, she had been giving little hints; such as "Seen any ghosts lately, big boy?"

But it was still Luka's nature to be determinedly independent, and he tried to shrug off those little hints.

Eve was realizing that she would need to be more blunt.

"I hope you don't have a gun, Luka. Or next time you mistake me for a monster, I might be a dead one."

Of course, like nearly any Montana boy, Luka did have a gun. He had two, in fact: A 12-gauge shot gun, and a 22-caliber rifle. Both had been given to him by his father – and they were just standard equipment for hunting, or for dealing with pesky varmints like skunks in those parts.

"I get the point, My Sweet. I don't think I'd ever shoot you. I haven't thought about shooting anything for a long time . . . But I guess I really don't know what my mind is doing sometimes now."

"And you admit that the hallucinations have been getting worse?" Eve asked, with a determined look of inquiry in her furrowed brow.

Luka could not lie to Eve. And he knew he shouldn't be trying to run away from the problem either. He should be more like her – facing any challenge head on.

"Yes, that seems to be true," he finally admitted.

"Thanks for being honest, with me – and with yourself," was her reply.

Then she added, "Do you think it's time to call the surgeon? . . . Is it time to start that treatment he told us about? Before it's too late?"

"You know what, my love? I guess it is . . . while I can still think straight."

And now Luka was smiling. And for so many reasons.

Eve would put in the call to the surgeon the next day.

Jen-Jen was surprised to learn that Brando was back in town. They had all assumed that he would either FREEZE completely to death out there this time . . . or come back with that Indian princess on his arm.

Yes, they had all heard the story of Brando's colorful "escape" from the county hospital, and the eloquent words he'd left them with: "She will CARE for me now. . . And we will be taking our LEAVE this hour."

True enough, they still thought that Brando was a bit whacked. What else could they think? Building that giant outdoor theater in the middle of nowhere?

They were half right. Upon returning, he did have that Indian princess on his arm.

But he was not back to introduce them to Stacy. Nor to report that they were invited to a wedding.

All of that may happen . . . later.

All in due time.

But, as always, Brando had LARGER dramatics in mind just now.

He also had Stacy backing him up at this point. His Indian princess cared nothing for introductions, but she WAS into Brando and his dream.

Just as she had upon making her strident entrance into the hospital (where she claimed Brando), Stacy had something to say.

> "This man is right. People NEED big stories, big stories they can see . . . outside under the sky. We will build his place to make those stories LIVE."

Jen-Jen was quite taken with all of this. She could see that Brando and Stacy had something special going.

And maybe that outdoor amphitheater wasn't such a crazy idea, after all. People did love stories, and Montana was the right place to perform them in a BIG way.

Just like balloon rides out over the magnificent tundra, a giant amphitheater out there was a fittingly Montana-sized project.

All it needed was the right marketing.

Once Jen's mind was ON it, she started to see promoting that giant amphitheater as a boon for Rod as well. Yes, it would be a DOUBLE win. Why? Because it would help to promote Rod's balloon ride business, as he could ferry more and more people out just to SEE that grand theater, and not just when a performance was underway.

That outdoor pavilion was a WONDER in its own right, a testament to the wonders of humanness – the same humanness that certain traditions had done their utmost to besmirch and condemn as inherently banal and evil.

Like the rest of Western Montana, that giant theater carved out of the side of a mountain was a sight to see.

Jen's plan worked like a charm, a charm *in duplicate*. Soon people were calling Rod's number every day for balloon rides out to see that wonder. Rod was off to a great start in his new business.

And the more Rod's business thrived, the more publicity it meant for Brando's dream.

"Hey, Jen-Jen," Rod suggested one day, "Selling those cosmetics is just making OTHER people money. You should start you own marketing company."

Jen's last name was Keith, like Toby Keith. Well, Jen was fine with that name. But "The Keith Agency" didn't have a Western ring to it.

So instead it became: "**The Double J** Marketing Agency: We'll Brand You With Success."

That had the Western flavor Jen wanted. And she delivered as advertised.

It was 6 weeks later.

Six weeks ago Luka had started his immunotherapy. Although the treatments had not stopped his mental decline, and the prognosis had only gotten worse, he had risen to the occasion.

And Eve was proud of him.

So was everyone else in their circle of friends and family. Despite Luka having passed away, he had done so gracefully; with nary a complaint -- and smiling with his last breath.

For nearly a month after Luka's passing, Eve had felt almost nothing. That is called "shock," the first stage of grief.

The greater the loss to the aggrieved one left behind, the greater the love, the longer that first stage lasts. The next stage is anger, and Eve had yet to finish with that.

In those early weeks, she had doubted that she'd even bother with the race. When it wasn't the numbness of shock, she had felt only anger – or despair.

But the stages of grief overlap at times, and Eve had seen glimpses of something approaching "resolution." As is always the case, what works best is not to, in any way, try to minimize or find a "bright side" to the loss – but to *memorialize* the person.

He was still a part of her – and she kept hearing him insist that she would amaze them all.

He – or his soul – was still excited for her.

And now Eve had reverted to form. She was determined again – *determined not to disappoint Luka.*

It was race day, and they were all in a good mood. That good mood was part of the benefit we all enjoy when we've been able to help others, especially when those others really NEED it. And TMK's team knew they had been highly successful in their local contribution to the statewide charity drive. They had been SO successful . . . that they had each received phone calls from the Governor's Office congratulating them.

Upon TMK's request, in Luka's place, the Governor's office had called "Reggie," Luka's father, to extend congratulation's, condolences and a "post-humous **commendation** to your brave son, who somehow managed to make a such a noble contribution in the face of his life-threatening circumstances." A certificate of honor would follow in the mail.

Now everyone in their circle was there, gathered in the best center-of-the-track seats, purchased early, to see Eve race.

In the time trials the day before, Eve had earned a front-row position – not the most desirable INSIDE position. But it was in the front row, and no one was in her way.

When the flag went down, Eve shot out to the lead. Still leading when she reached that first corner, Rusty yelled, "Lean hard, Eve. Make 'em eat lots of your snow."

As a one-time racer himself, Rusty knew what he was talking about. When you are ahead in a corner, throwing up lots of snow makes it hard for those chasing after . . . hard for them to SEE you, or where they are going.

Eve remained ahead coming down that first full straightaway, and TMK roared "Hammer down, Eve. Let her rip." Teresa, now with a wink to her husband, couldn't resist a little side comment, "But don't fly into the STANDS like you know who."

Teresa's remark was made only under her breath; no one heard it but Rusty; indeed, she was barely able to get the words out of her mouth . . . in the midst of trying to stifle one of her just-too-charming giggles.

Rusty didn't seem to mind. People were always teasing him like that; probably because he took it so well. And this was no exception, as he answered Teresa only by a double thumbs up gesture, and broadening his trademark smirk.

Still, Eve may have overpowered into the turn at the end of that straightaway, going higher on the banked corner than she might have wished, and one of her competitors slipped under and passed her on the inside.

"Go GET that weasel," screamed Michelle, as Eve came out of the turn. Yes, even demure and refined damsels like TMK's Michelle, could get caught up such a spectacle.

And why not?

It was a 120-lap race, 20 laps longer than the standard for the snowmobile circuit. That might – and probably did – speak to an issue of ENDURANCE. But, as Rusty had put it for Montana as a whole, The Big Sky Challenge *was not for wimps.*

Everyone was reminded of that fact in the tense moments following 3 separate crashes, each stopping the race for a while – and requiring officials to do restarts, with each racer in his or her proper position before the flag went down again.

On one of those occasions, a racer left on a gurney, with the medics attending him first – and the wail of the ambulance as it left bespeaking the risks of the sport loudly and clearly.

But there was no daunting the spirits of the enclave there in support of the hometown hero. Eve was no wimp, as they all knew. She would lose the lead but then regain it several times in course of the grueling race.

No matter. Whether it was her light weight, an endurance advantage, her determination, or the crowd being clearly on her side, Eve started to pull away near the end. When the checkered flag waved as the hometown favorite crossed the finish line, she was more than half a lap ahead of them all.

Luka's prediction had prevailed.

The sponsors and promotors of The Big Sky Challenge were not about to skimp on the prizes they presented to the winner and top placers in their *"first annual spectacle on runners."*

The trophy was nearly as tall as Eve herself.

A portable stand was quickly brought to the center of the main straightaway, site of both the starting and the finish line. As Eve was called to the stand, her fans were now cheering SO loudly that the announcer had to wave his hands downward in front of the microphone as he called, "Please . . . we need to hold it down a bit . . . so we can hear what the winner has to say."

The crowd obliged the announcer, and they all heard Eve declare, "I will have this trophy inscribed for the man who inspired me to win it. It will read, *'For Luka, the love of my life.'*"

Yes, that could prove difficult to explain to any *new* man, any suiter who might hope to win Eve's heart in the future. But to borrow from the most famous line of Margaret Mitchell's immortal "Gone With The Wind" (New York: Macmillan,1936), frankly, my dears, Eve didn't give a Damn!

ABOUT THE AUTHOR

Ron Neff (Ph.D University of Iowa) is a semi-retired professor and psychotherapist. In recent years he has published several self-help books: Goodbye, My Love: How To Mend A Broken Heart (2016), Loving Well: Keys to Lasting and Rewarding Relationships (2016), and Your Inner Mammal: How To Meet Your Real Emotional Needs And Become Stronger - For Self And Others (2017). He has often been told he should write novels, probably love stories, since he has studied and worked with issues of the heart most of his life. Hence, The Color of the Moon (2017), Daisies in Hell (2019), One Heart Over the Line (2019), Heroes, Hellions and Hot Rods (2019) and Enough With Those Humans (2020). But now an inspirational tale of larger than life souls; heroes – both male and female – with more than just love on their minds.

Ingram Content Group UK Ltd.
Milton Keynes UK
UKHW042025080323
418284UK00005B/21